E.L. REED

ELRpublishing

Published by ELR Publishing.

ISBN-13: 978-1-944550-14-1

Cover and interior design by Kenny Holcomb
kennyholcomb@gmail.com

Printed in the United States of America

To Harleigh

May your smile always light the world around you

prologue

Two years prior…

I had just been hired at this quaint bed-and-breakfast. The inn was just getting ready to open for the upcoming season, and today I had the opportunity to get familiar with my new place. I was giddy with excitement to start this new journey.

I explored the second floor, peeking in at all the rooms. Then I went to the first floor and checked out the back rooms off the kitchen. There were three bedrooms and a storage room; me, the housekeeper, and the cook would sleep here. Off the main foyer—where the registration desk stood—was a living room where a fireplace was in the center of two, floor-to-ceiling bookcases. The living room on the backside of the house had ceiling-to-floor windows that opened onto a deck overlooking the ocean. The deck was going to be my favorite place. I just knew it.

I moved to the other side of the foyer. One room on this main floor was positioned almost under the stairs, but extended away from the house. The owner had instructed that this particular room was not to be used unless the inn was full.

I wandered in and glanced around. The room was small, but it had a spectacular view from the windows. I would consider this the best room in the house. I curiously moved around it. The closet was long, as opposed to *wide*, which seemed odd, but it went under the stair access, so I assumed that was the reason. I adjusted some hangers on the rack.

As I turned to step back out of the closet, my toe caught on a bump in the floor. I bent to inspect it and found a small section of the flooring that did not fit into the tongue and groove. I tried to push it in, and when I couldn't budge it, I pulled it up. The floor lifted as one piece in a large square in my hand and revealed a trap door. I pushed the section of floor back out of the way and opened the trap door. I held my breath, expecting a large creak as the door pulled up.

Silence.

I grabbed my cell phone to turn on the flashlight and peered down. Stone stairs descended circularly. I couldn't see beyond that. I heard Minnie, the house-keeper, who crept around silently—hence the mousy nickname—moving around in the living room. It spurred me to put the trap door back down and pull the flooring into place. I made a mental note to get a small runner over this flooring section to keep a guest from tripping over it.

I decided to make a return trip tonight to explore what was below the room. A chill of excitement ran through me, and an unexplained feeling of déjà vu came over me. I shook my head and headed for the living room.

The day dragged on as I helped Minnie with the bedrooms, prepping for the five rooms that would be used tomorrow night. I then checked on Ramsay in the kitchen to see if he was prepared for the cocktail hour, offered with small hors d'oeuvres and breakfast. It was the understanding of the guests arriving that if they wished to order dinner some night, they needed to give twenty-four-hours' notice for the meal, otherwise, after cocktails and hors d'oeuvres, they would go into town to eat at a local restaurant.

After Minnie and Ramsay, the cook, had gone to bed, and I knew they would be asleep, I crept out of my room and made my way to Room 1. I carried a pair of sneakers in my hand to put on in the room. I didn't know what to expect at the bottom of those stairs.

With shoes on and the trap door open, I pulled out my cell phone and flipped on the flashlight. I cautiously started down the stone stairs. The walls, also made of stone, were rough as I ran my hand along the wall while descending the circular stairway. It had no railing, and the stone was cold under my fingers. The air got colder and damper the farther down I went. When I arrived at the bottom of the stairs, I saw a short hallway leading to a door to my left. Straight across from the stairs was a room. As I stepped into it, an icy feeling ran over me, and I shivered from the intensity of it.

This room had tracks on the floor, a hose to one side, and a table on the back wall. Next to the table was another door. I went to it first and opened it. It was a closet lined with empty, dusty shelves. They obviously hadn't been used for a long time. I turned toward the bench and saw a box with a red button on it. I picked it up and pushed the button. A small whirling sound startled me, and I spun around to find spikes rising out of the floor.

A stabbing pain shot through my head above my eyes, and I dropped the controller. It landed with a clatter, snapping me out of the pain. I bent to pick it up. As I rose and set it on the table, I studied the bed of spikes. There were five strategically placed, with three in a row and two more that were spread out lower than the lined ones and laid out perpendicularly to the others. I walked around them and noticed on the floor, not only the tracks where the bed of spikes could come out or nest back in there, but also a drainage hole where water could drain.

I shook my head. A feeling of giddiness overtook me as a flash of a young man lying on those spikes, *dead*, invaded my mind. I stared at the sharp, lethal points and carefully ran my hand down one of the iron rods. I glanced up at the ceiling above the spikes and saw where there was a section cut out with hinges to the side like that of a door.

I had such a feeling of familiarity in this place, yet I shook it off. Before I left the room, I pushed the button to lower the spikes back into the floor. I went to the door at the end of the hallway and opened it, discovering a small path between the cliff and the house. I closed the door again.

Hmm. . .

I contemplated all I'd seen and retraced my steps back upstairs. This job just got a whole lot more interesting.

one

The sun was just beginning to set when the young man walked in. He had that travel-fatigue look. He was tall and athletic, with blue eyes and dark hair. The man probably stopped traffic. He was so gorgeous. I smiled and felt a blush spread across my cheeks.

"Good evening, sir," I greeted him.

"Good evening. Do you have any vacancies?" He smiled.

"Yes. Will it be just you?"

"Yes, ma'am." He reached behind him, grabbed his billfold, and yanked out a credit card. "Just one night, please."

I processed the card and watched him glance around. "What brings you to Madison, Charles?"

"Please, call me Charlie. I've walked the Shoreline Greenway Trail. A friend of mine told me it was a great walk and said I should take my time and do it in a couple of days." He wrapped his fingers around the strap of his backpack, still on his shoulder. "Hence, the light travel. I'd thought I would stop for the night, and then walk the eight hours tomorrow back to my car."

"Have you had a chance to eat? I can make you up a sandwich with something to drink."

"That would be great. I'd like that."

I made a note of it and handed back his credit card. "Your room is Room 1." I pointed at the door to the right of the stairs. "You can drop off your bag, and I'll put in the food order. Come out and eat on the back porch."

He gestured to the French doors just beyond the stairway. "Right there on the back porch?"

"Yes, sir. Just go ahead right out there and pick a table."

He nodded and started toward his room. The house was old and huge, but the view of the ocean was incredible and well worth the upkeep.

I went to the kitchen and ordered the man a sandwich and iced tea. The deck was my favorite spot. The smell of the ocean, watching the water. There was nothing more relaxing.

"This is amazing," he said as I set the tray down on a table. He turned from the railing where he had been looking out at the ocean.

"Yes, the view never gets old." I waited until he sat. "Just let me know if there is anything else I can get you."

"Stay. Tell me about this place." He stood up, indicating I should sit.

Once I lowered myself into the chair, he returned

to his seat. "Well, this building has been standing here for well over a hundred years. It's different from most, with a stone basement. The upstairs was renovated a few years ago to accommodate more guests. In the summer, we're pretty packed. However, you came at a great time. It's quieter but will pick up in the next couple of weeks as the foliage really takes on color."

"You run it alone?"

I hesitated a moment. "I'm just the hostess. Moved here for a change of scenery after my fiancé and I called things off."

"I take it he decided it wasn't his thing." Charlie sounded sincere, and yet I bristled at the sound of his words.

I shook my head slowly. "What about you? You're traveling alone."

Charlie sat back, having cleaned his plate, and took another drink of the tea. It was half gone at this point. "Yeah, I'm by myself. Decided it was time for me to get out there after breaking up with my girlfriend about a year ago. You know how it is… plenty of fish in the sea, or so they say."

My back stiffened as the words hit me. Why? Why did he have to say those words? "Anything else I can get you?" I asked as I stood and reached for his empty plate.

"Maybe a refill on this tea that I can take to my room." He handed me his glass.

I nodded and went to refill his glass, but I paused in the kitchen, having poured the tea. My hand shook as I dispensed in a few drops of my special ingredient. The time had come for the moment of truth. Doubts flooded my mind. Had I gotten the ratios right? Despite the doubts, my heart raced with the excitement of seeing how this played out.

I heard the French doors shut as Charlie came back into the house. I met him at the foot of the stairs and handed him the glass. After he shut the door to his room, I stood at the railing outside and watched the colorful sky fade into the night. His room overlooked the ocean, and I could see the shadow of him moving about inside it.

A smile tugged at the corner of my mouth. The anticipation was building, and I forced myself not to rush it. I would wait for the cover of darkness and the little light the moon gave off. It wouldn't matter if he had fallen asleep or not, he wouldn't be moving or saying anything. I knew from experience that if the tea was drunk right down, it would paralyze him within twenty minutes. However, most patrons took their time, and it could be an hour before he was ready for me.

I glanced at my watch as the moon rose to its place, and the light glinted off the water. It was time. He had shut his light off earlier. I waited outside his door and listened.

No sound.

I unlocked the door and slowly turned the handle, quietly pushing the door open. He was lying on the bed, seemingly asleep. His eyes flickered open as I approached the bed. I took in the empty glass on the nightstand and smiled.

He tried to speak, but the paralytic had done its

job and rendered him helpless. The once-powerful man was now at my mercy.

This was my favorite part. These men would always glance around rapidly, and then try to stare me down.

I shook my head. Why would I think that? I'd never killed before, yet the words in my mind felt like a memory. It faded and I just stood there quietly next to him, watching. His eyes became panicked as he tried to move his arms and legs. The realization that he was immobile caused even more terror to fill his eyes.

I patted his hand gently, then leaned down and whispered into his ear. "Plenty of fish in the sea. *You* will be one of the fish in the sea." I opened the tiny box I carried with me and pulled out a fishhook that had a bright blue feather attached to it. "It matches your eyes." I opened his mouth just a little and pushed the barbed hook into his cheek near his mouth. I tugged it a bit to see the pain in his eyes. "Did I hook you? Or are you still ready to see all the other fish in the sea?"

I reached behind the headboard and pushed the small button invisible to anyone who didn't know it existed.

Whoosh!

The bottom of the bed collapsed under him, falling to the left of the pit that lay beneath the bedframe. The light illuminated the iron spikes at the bottom of the hole. They were on a motion sensor, so when the bed collapsed, they automatically came on, allowing me to watch my victory. I smiled as he fell and landed on the spikes, impaling him. There were only a few spikes, but their strategic placement allowed them to penetrate his neck and torso. Sometimes death wasn't immediate.

I moved to the closet, pulled open the trap door, and descended to the lower floor.

Somewhat satisfied, I walked around my victim and watched the red blood run down the spikes onto the floor. It mesmerized me how it pooled beneath him in some areas, and in others, it dripped through the cracks under the spikes. They were on a track where I could retract them into the floor with the push of a button, enabling me to easily remove the body without the hindrance of the sharp protrusions.

This man was a masterpiece. I circled around him again, enjoying the view. I retracted the spikes, and the thud of the body hitting the floor heightened my senses. The man wasn't quite dead yet, and his eyes revealed pain and fear. The fear was always a good sign. This man, when walking through my door, hadn't been on my radar as my next victim. But then, he went and was so flippant about all the *fish in the sea*. Men like him couldn't be allowed to live. They threw women away just to move on to the next one.

He brought it on himself; I rationalized.

Blood continued to pool next to him, and I leaned down to consider his eyes. He had incredible blue eyes; ones I would want to gaze into for the rest of my life. Yes, they were my trophy. I stood and went to the side table and reached for the enucleation spoon and scissors. I allowed the last bit of life to leave him before I performed the removal of Charlie's eyeballs. I picked them up carefully. While holding them gingerly, I took a small hypodermic needle. I injected alcohol into several locations of each eyeball before placing them in a jar of alcohol to save them until I was ready. I laid down a piece of plastic, rolled the body onto it, and wrapped it up tight. I then rolled him into a large storage bag—the kind usually used to hold a Christmas tree. I zipped it up and sprayed a sealant along the zipper so water wouldn't get into it.

I dragged the bag out the back door and along the path. As the path ended at the edge of the lawn, I pulled the bag over the grass toward the old well. It had not been used in years as it had become contaminated by saltwater coming in from the ocean somehow. It didn't matter to me why it wasn't being used, just that because of that fact, it was the perfect spot to hide a body. Eventually, with the dry well, I could burn them, but there was no hurry. The bags would cover any odor that the body gave off.

I walked over to the body's feet and lifted. It took some doing, but I managed to get the body up on the well side and push it over the edge. There was a slight splash as the heavy bag hit the bottom that had some water in it. Something tugged at my heart as I wondered why this one had to be so insensitive. But then, lately, all the good-looking ones were. They had no heart; no thought of the callus remarks they made in passing.

Once back inside, I pulled out the hose and started washing down the floor. There was a drain in the stone floor, and the blood and water would eventually make its way into the depths of the dirt beneath the stone basement.

I pushed the button to raise the spikes back up for the next victim, then rinsed the blood off them and squeegeed the standing water to the drain. I surveyed the room. Ready once again. I opened the concealed door in the wall and revealed shelves that held various jars. Some were empty, and others contained unique items: cat eyes, a raccoon's tongue. My experiments until I could get it right. More recent jars held fingers and thumbs, as well as toes. These blue eyes were exactly what I needed to make my masterpiece.

I went up the stairs, closed the trap door, and reset the bed. This room would need to be purged of any personal items. The backpack on the chair caught my eye. I grabbed it, mentally making a note to go through it and make sure Charlie didn't have a phone or had called anyone. As I locked the door behind me, tiredness hit, and I was finally ready for bed.

two

Dawson walked toward the shore and glanced around the crowd of people that had gathered. The local police had corded off the area and were doing their best to keep the locals out. Still, cameras were going off, and people had their phones out recording. He ducked under the yellow tape, and without saying a word, walked to the body lying at the edge of the water. A tarp half-covered the body.

"Do we have an ID yet?" Dawson spoke to the man in uniform on his right. Dawson pulled his coat collar up to block some of the winter. It was a chilly morning. Late fall on the ocean was never a warm time of year.

"No, sir."

Dawson cringed at the word, *sir*. God, he hated that, but it was to be expected when working with the local offices. At the State Police headquarters, he was never called sir. Last name only, and everyone knew he preferred it that way. After working with him on the Lizzie Borden Case, he still heard from Officer Brown from the Leighton Police Department. The man had been helpful during that investigation. Still, even Brown had learned to drop the sir after a while.

Dawson crouched beside the body and lifted the plastic tarp. He threw up a silent prayer that this wouldn't be another chase after a ghost. The man's body rested partially inside some kind of storage bag. Dawson carefully pulled it open to find that the man was wearing boxers and nothing else. At least, the cold water had helped preserve the body.

Dawson moved around him. He had wounds on the body that could have come from being in the water, beating him against rocks or the seabed. At a closer look, there appeared to be holes in his torso, but what caused them would have to be for Ali to answer. The one thing that stuck out as odd was the fishhook in the man's cheek. It had a blue feather on the end.

"Detective Dawson?" A deep voice came from behind him, and he turned as he stood up to see the Branford Police Chief standing there.

"Yes, sir." Dawson reached out to shake the chief's hand. "Wes Dawson."

"Welcome. I'm Tony Harris. We've got a space at the station if you want to set up a base camp. I'll have a couple of my guys work with you if you need it." He gestured to the body. "Any clues about what we've got here?"

"More than a dead body, nothing yet. He has some puncture-type wounds that the ME will need to clarify, and the fishhook in the mouth. Not sure if it's anything more than an accidental fishing accident."

Dawson relaxed as he saw the ME van drive up. Ali stepped out and grabbed her bag. She picked her way down to the water's edge. "What do you know so far?" she asked as she came to stand next to Dawson.

"Not much. Some odd-looking open old marks, punctures of some sort. From the hook in his mouth, first impression would be a fishing accident."

Ali nodded and squatted next to the body. She pulled on a pair of gloves and reached out to look at one wound on his chest. He knew the bloating didn't help with distinguishing what had caused it. "I'll have to get him back to the morgue and start the autopsy before I can give you any actual information."

Dawson acknowledged her comment and sighed. "It's one body, so that's something."

Ali glanced at him. "Not every dead body is going to be from a serial killer."

"I know." He shrugged and turned toward a young officer taking pictures. "Make sure I get a copy of those pictures at the station."

"Yes, sir," the officer replied. Dawson rolled his eyes, and he could hear Ali's light chuckle behind him.

"Wes." Ali's voice was soft, but held a touch of concern.

He turned to look at her, and she gestured him closer. As he bent down to hear her, she pointed at the victim's face.

"Eyeballs are gone. At first glance, because the eyelids are intact, I would say they were removed. I'll look more in depth back at the morgue."

Dawson sighed. "If someone had deliberately removed them, I have a feeling there will be more bodies."

Ali nodded. "I'm afraid so. Let's hope not, but…"

Dawson walked along the edge of the water in both directions from where the body had been found. He discovered nothing else out of the ordinary, but it gave him a moment to organize his thoughts. He had taken some time off after the Lizzie Borden Case with the hatchet. It had been a stressful investigation, besides long nights still searching for his sister.

Frustration with his sister always ran high in him, even more so every time she left him a note telling him to stop searching for her. He couldn't let it go. He didn't want her out there alone, and he needed her to know he was there for her and wanted her off the streets. If he could just figure out why Sara was doing this to *him*, the one person in her life who'd always stood by her.

Dawson started to his car. Might as well get set up at the local precinct and get this investigation started. Something in the pit of his stomach told him this would not be an open-and-shut case. He exhaled slowly and turned toward the local police, still packing up their things.

three

Ali stood over the body and studied it carefully before touching it. The body obviously had been in cold water by the adipocere covering it. This *grave wax* helped preserve the body and inhibited the growth of bacteria, as well as being sealed in a heavy canvas bag, making it almost impossible to determine how long it had been in the water at this point.

With gloves on, Ali prodded at the wounds. They went straight through, and there was a total of five going from the neck, down the man's torso, with one through each leg. The back of the head was intact. She gently pulled back the eyelids and saw that someone had clipped the tendons around the eyes instead of being eaten away by sea critters. She made notes as she worked. The bag he had been in had done a good job of preserving the body, really. Water had seeped into the canvas material, but the zipper had been sealed so no water could get in. Even the canvas material should have been waterproof, but even that could allow water seepage after so long.

The hook in the man's cheek seemed like an odd thing to have. She looked closely at the barb inserted from the outside of the cheek. She didn't know enough about fishing to know if this could have been accidental hooking from a fishing accident. However, with the missing eyeballs, Ali leaned more toward homicide. She continued through the autopsy and slid the body into the locker.

As she washed her hands, she started forming her report in her mind. By the time she sat down at her desk, she was in an excellent spot to type her findings. She pushed away from the never-ending pile of files, labeled a new file folder, and opened the report form on her computer. She typed up the report and sat back when she got to where she needed the cause of death. This wasn't a fishing accident. She was positive and needed to code it as a homicide. She sighed and prayed that this would not be the beginning of another killing spree. However, the timeline was off with the death being anywhere from a handful of months to weeks. She couldn't put an exact time of death on this one. And they had no identity so far. She would wait on dental impressions to hopefully get a positive ID.

She grabbed her cell phone and typed out a text to Wes: *homicide, no ID yet.*

She felt like she was constantly the bearer of bad news in this job, and it wore on her. Though definitely not as much as it wore on Wes and his career. He carried the weight of the world on his shoulders between the job and looking for his sister.

Dawson walked into the Branford Police Station and looked around. He noticed Captain Harris in his office, so Dawson approached the door and knocked on the door frame.

"Dawson, come on in."

"Thank you, sir." Dawson stepped into the office.

"Well, that surprises me." Harris chuckled.

"Excuse me?" Dawson questioned.

"I've heard rumors you hate being addressed as sir, and yet here you use that *sir* crap on me."

Dawson laughed. "I guess I did."

"Here, please, call me Harris. I prefer just the last name, as I assume you also do. Something about a military background."

Mention of the military caused Dawson to stiffen a moment before he relaxed back into the banter. After he had screwed up his knee, the medical discharge from the service had left him bitter for a while. He still had pangs of guilt for not finishing out his time in the service with his buddies who were out there putting their life on the line all the time, and he was stuck here at home searching out killers. Somehow, in his mind, it just wasn't the same.

"What do you need from us, Dawson?" Harris asked.

"A small room to set up my investigation. I'm a visual person, so I'd like a board to work off. And, more importantly, some decent coffee."

"I've got one of the conference rooms set up for you with a chalkboard that on the reverse has a corkboard. As for coffee, it depends on who makes it, which will determine if it's decent or barely tolerable."

Dawson shook his head. "What is about police departments that no one can make a decent pot of coffee?"

Harris grinned. "Head this way. I'll show you where you'll be. Just let me know if you need some extra hands. I can spare a couple of guys to help you out, but like more departments, we've had budget cuts, so we're working on a minimal crew."

"Seems to happen everywhere," Dawson commiserated. The captain and Dawson entered the conference room, and Dawson looked around. As promised, there was a roller board that had both chalk and corkboard depending on the side. Dawson turned it so the corkboard was visible.

Dawson glanced at his phone. The text from Ali was brief, but to the point. Damn, homicide. He had known it in his gut but hoped for something easy that would only take a few days to get through. He sighed and decided to make a pot of coffee. He wanted and *needed* a decent cup that was more than just tolerable.

"Looks like we'll need to be having a press conference. It's important that we get some information out there, so hopefully, someone will come forward with some information on this victim. Medical examiner says homicide." Dawson turned toward Captain Harris.

"I'll get one set up for later this afternoon. I'll let you know the time as soon as I know." Captain Harris left the room before Dawson could respond. Within a couple of hours, Harris had told Dawson the press would be out front in five minutes. Dawson sat down to prepare what he was about to say.

Once in front of the cameras, Dawson cleared his throat and began.

"A body has been found on Branford Beach. At this time, we have not identified the victim, but believe this to be a homicide. We are asking for your help. If you know of any persons missing, or other information that could lead to an identification of the body and help in the investigation, please call the number on the screen. We have a team ready to take your calls and follow up on any leads that come in. I will not be taking questions at this time as we are at the start of the investigation and have nothing yet to share with the public." This news broadcast was being sent out across the state, not just the city or county, which hopefully would generate some sort of response.

four

I stared at the small TV in my room. The news had just said they had found a body and were looking for information on a missing person. My heart stopped. I needed to check the well to see if it was my body or if it was somebody else. I couldn't think of what would happen if my body had somehow gotten out of the well.

I laughed to myself at the absurdity of the idea.

My mind whirled at the prospect of where I could dispose of the bodies now that the first one had been found so quickly, if it was, in fact, my body. Thankfully, tomorrow I had the morning off, and I would scout the area. I needed to think of preserving the bodies just in case I ended up needing more parts. One never knew what I could salvage after the fact, and when I thought more clearly after the adrenaline from the kill had subsided.

The next morning, I got up early. There had been no guests the night before, so I had a free morning before I needed to be back to greet new arrivals. Last night, I had done some online searching of the area for what could be potential spots to dispose of bodies, but also to keep my trophies to share with the man I knew would be in my life soon. First, I needed to see if something had actually happened with the well.

It was early and no one else was up, so I grabbed a flashlight and went out to the well. I shined the light down, and I could see the bottom with a small amount of water, but no bag with the body I had tossed down there. As I tried to see more, it looked like water was moving. My light caught a shadow, or a darker area, to the side. I changed my position to get a better view, and sure enough, water was coming in through a hole in the ground near the bottom of the well. Could the body have left the well and ended up in the sea?

I tried looking over the cliff but couldn't see anything. I'd need a boat to get in close if I truly wanted to know if there was a hole coming from the well to the ocean. However, at this point, knowing the body was no longer at the bottom of the well, I needed a Plan B.

I spent the next few hours searching the neighboring towns for areas that could be useful. I found a couple of possibilities, but needed to research the use of them before I could commit. Out of the way, abandoned areas were the best, but there also needed to be some sort of temperature control… A way of freezing the bodies so they would last longer, and that handsome detective could not get his hands on them so easily.

But I also needed a workspace, away from the prying eyes of my coworkers. My mind went to the house that I had grown up in. I doubted my brother would be there now, since he hadn't texted saying he would be. He only stayed there when he was around, and he was gone traveling most of the time. After our parents died, I never looked back on the place. I hadn't seen my brother in years and preferred it that way. Why he still let me know his whereabouts, or how he wanted to get together when he came to town, always surprised me, but right now, that worked in my favor. I knew he was currently out of state and would be gone for the next few months.

I turned my car toward Lyme, the small town that I'd grown up in, and headed for my parents' house on the outskirts of the town. Their wooded five acres of land might be perfect for me. When I drove down the driveway, and the house came into sight, I slowed the car. Not much had changed in the time I had been gone. My brother obviously hadn't remodeled it much, at least on the outside.

I parked the car and walked up to the front porch. The key was still under the potted plant by the front door. My brother always reminded me it was there. He wanted me back here, at least to visit. I let myself in. I stopped just inside the door and closed my eyes. I had excellent memories of my childhood until my parents died and my fiancé dumped me. I opened my eyes and moved farther into the house. The living room was right inside the door. My brother had changed very little. Same furniture, in the exact place as when we were kids. I suppose when you aren't home much, you just keep things the same.

I moved on to the kitchen. Again, nothing had changed. I wandered around, ventured upstairs to my old bedroom. I had loved this place, yet coming back to it, I felt nothing. No flashes of memories that I had expected. Lately, all my flashes of memories seemed to belong to someone else… visions of things I couldn't place or seem to remember.

As I stood in my bedroom and looked out my window at the view of the back of the house, I saw the barn. We never had animals and remembered being told to stay out of it as "it wasn't safe." I could remember my father spending time out there, though. I never questioned why *we* shouldn't go out there, and now, the sight of it sparked my curiosity.

I left the house and walked across the back yard to the barn. The door still had the same old padlock, rusted now, and I easily broke it off with a crowbar I found at the side of the barn. When I opened the doors, it took my eyes a moment to adjust to the darkness. I pulled out my phone and turned on the flashlight. It wasn't completely dark, but I needed a light so I wouldn't trip over anything. I moved farther in. It was constructed as any barn with horse stalls to one side. The other side had what could probably be used as a tack room, although a work bench ran along the back wall of it.

I moved over to the steps that went up to the hayloft. I placed my feet cautiously on the first few steps. They seemed sturdy enough, although it had been sitting there unused for many years. I watched carefully for rot as I moved upward, staying close to the railing in case I needed to grab it. Coming up to the loft, I stopped.

What?

All kinds of chains and shackles had been hooked to the walls. This was no ordinary loft. I moved around the room, examining everything. What was this place? What had my father been into? It looked more like a dungeon, except it was on the second floor of the barn, as opposed to being underground.

Was this where my deviant mind came from? Could my father have had the same demented brain? Maybe my visions were more from my childhood than I realized. Maybe I had actually known more about my father's doings and had blocked them out until I found the lovely room at the inn with the spikes.

I went back downstairs. I walked around the main floor of the barn again, this time keeping my eyes fastened on the floor. Could there be a trap door with another level that no one knew about? My thoughts went to the padlock. I'd need to re- place that, even though I doubted my brother ever ventured out there by the sight of the lock being so rusted. It probably hadn't been opened since my father was living.

In the tack room, I found what I was looking for. In the darkest corner of the room, I spotted a small ring in the floor. Dirt had accumulated over the years, so I brushed it away, and I could open the trap door. Excitement coursed through me as I pulled the door up and peered down. I descended the first few steps and noticed the wall next to the stairs was cement. It was unheard of for a barn to have a foundation. When I reached the bottom of the steps, I realized it *wasn't* a foundation, but a small room with cement walls. It couldn't have been more than 12x12, and from what I could gather, it was only under the tack room.

I shone my flashlight around and saw another door at the opposite end of the stairs. I walked over and found it to be made of metal. I turned the handle and opened it. An overwhelming odor hit me. It smelled like something had been rotting for years there. I swept my flashlight around the small area and saw hooks from the ceiling. It was metal throughout and looked more like a meat locker. We never had animals that we killed for food, so I didn't know what this would have been used for. Did my father even know about this small room, this whole basement room? Although I couldn't see anything in the room that would cause the rotting smell, the floor looked dirty.

I left the door open and decided that I would need to come back with a better light to really find out more about the room and its use, but it drew me to it. Something in my mind triggered voices and memories. I tried to get up the stairs and close the trap door before the full onset hit me.

This is it. Exactly what we need.

The man's voice had come back. Who was it? My father?

I closed the doors of the barn as I exited and put the broken padlock back through the clasp. I needed *spikes*

a storage place before I could bring them here. One of the earlier sites would work out. I would make some calls when I got back to the inn to make sure it wouldn't be a problem.

five

I sat outside, staring out into the ocean, and my mind drifted to the past few months. They'd been slow, not only because of winter but also a down surge in the economy. The inn barely kept the doors opened. I didn't know how I'd get through another year. If it didn't pick up soon, the owners would close the bed-and-breakfast, and I'd have to move elsewhere. I liked the layout of this place; and the secret room that allowed me to work on my project with no one knowing. Somewhere along the way, things had gone from bad to worse, and it was out of my control.

It brought a sense of loneliness that some days I just couldn't shake. It would take me back to the days when I had been engaged. I was ready to get married. When my parents had died, I was so depressed, there were times I could hardly function.

My fiancé just couldn't, or *wouldn't*, wait around. He was the one that first threw the adage, "there's plenty of fish in the sea," in my face. That phrase still made my blood boil every time I heard it. It was a cop-out people would say, who just didn't want to make a relationship work, or something they told people they felt weren't capable of being in a relationship.

I knew the perfect man was out there, and I'd find him some day. Maybe someday sooner than I expected. The doorbell pulled me from my rumination. As I opened the door, there stood a man who looked like he'd been walking for hours. He was disheveled, and his pants were covered with dirt, giving the impression he had just been working in a garden.

"Can I help you?" I asked.

"Are there any rooms available?"

I looked him up and down, then glanced beyond him. There was no car, and he carried no bags. "Yes. Unfortunately, the kitchen is closed, but there is a room available."

"Great. I just need it for the night."

"Come on in." I stepped back to allow the man to pass by. He stopped just inside and glanced down at his jeans. He hurried back out onto the porch and brushed off his pants the best he could to knock off the excess dirt.

"Sorry about that." He reentered, a little calmer, and waited patiently for me to move ahead of him to the sign-in desk.

"No worries." I held open the register so he could sign in. "You said just one night?"

"Yes, ma'am." He didn't explain his lack of belongings, and I didn't feel I could ask. I debated what room to put him in, and then I gave him the room behind the stairs. If used by guests, it was my favorite room, especially for the single men. However, there was something very different about this man. I couldn't put my finger on it, but something was off.

"Can I get you a drink? Even though the kitchen is closed, I can put together a sandwich if you're hungry."

"I'm fine, thank you. No need for you to go out of your way. A hot shower and a good night's sleep are all that I require." The man took the key and headed to his room. I kept my eyes on him, but said nothing.

I returned to the deck to watch the ocean. The night was silent, other than the soft splashes from the waves rolling against the rocks. They mesmerized me. The lulling sound lured me into my thoughts, allowing me to go into memories that I usually shoved away and refused to think about.

When I was dating Tom, before we were engaged, there was a moment that I was happy. And I thought he had been, too. I couldn't have been more wrong. He said he didn't want to wait around for me to straighten things out after my parents died. In reality, it was the perfect time for him to break things off to be with the other *woman* he was seeing. I grunted. She was barely a girl. I should have expected it, yet I didn't and was completely blindsided by it. On the heels of my parents dying, my thought was that he would be my rock; instead, he was the avalanche that crushed me.

The window opened from my visitor's bedroom.

His name was Thomas, and maybe that was why the memories came flooding back. I had hoped he'd want something to eat and drink, just for the mere fact that his name was too familiar, and I didn't want him there. I didn't want such painful memories returning. I tried to ignore them and live in my little bubble, where I focused just on myself and no one else.

I mentally dared this man to come out and reference all the fish in the sea. I wanted to put him to sleep in the ocean with the fishes. There was no way to get that started unless I could sneak into his room in a few hours and just drop the bed. However, it was risky if he wasn't paralyzed. He was a big man, and I couldn't afford to be overpowered by him. It would ruin everything I had worked toward so far.

In my mind, I went through the closet in the basement. I had always had a fascination with forensics and years ago, I decided to try my hand at it. I had started by finding dead animals and watched online videos on how to preserve things. As my knowledge grew, I began digging up graves and gathering fingers and toes, mostly which couldn't be used now. I used them to learn how to preserve body parts, and it had taken me some time to master, but I had the most gorgeous blue eyes sitting in a jar just waiting to finish my creation. Thomas would have been perfect for *some* part. I didn't know which one, but he was a handsome specimen.

My thoughts were interrupted when I heard the man talking...

He must be on the phone. I listened carefully.

"I know this is the place Charlie was at. He described the view that night he got here." There was silence for a few moments while he likely listened to the person on the other end of the phone.

"I just need to find something that proves he was here. I'll let you know what I find."

I clenched my fists at my side. So, this guy was looking for my blue-eyed friend. I slightly grinned as I thought about how Charlie was so close. *Part of him anyway.* Still, the grin quickly faded.

This could mean trouble, and I couldn't allow anything to be found that would show Charlie had been there. I'd taken the sim card of his phone that night, destroying both in the furnace as well as the man's backpack and clothes. There was no trace of him in this place.

I sat back and waited, willing the man to come out of his room and ask for something to drink. When he didn't appear, and I saw the light go out in his room, I contemplated my next move. I had a feeling he wasn't really going to sleep, not if he was hell-bent on finding something about his friend, Charlie.

I slowly stood and made my way to the main living room, just to the side of where I registered guests. I clicked off lights as I moved from the room and settled into a chair in the dark. I wasn't about to let this man snoop through my things, and if *I* was looking for someone, that would definitely be my course of action.

A couple of hours went by when I heard the soft click of his door opening. I sat quietly and just waited. A small lamp had been left on at the registration desk, so I could see if he approached it. I felt the tension tighten in my neck and the strain of my eyes as I waited for the first sight of him. Finally, he peeked around the staircase and crept to the registration desk. He was shoeless and padded across the floor in his socks. He glanced around the registration desk and opened the book that guests had signed. He flipped through and put it back.

I smiled. The book Charlie had signed had ended that night, and I had torn out the last page after carefully rewriting the few names before him. I burned the page with the rest of his belongings, but that book had already been locked away. I reached for the lamp beside me and pulled the chain to light up the room. "Is there something I can help you find?"

Thomas jumped and turned to face me. His face reddened at being caught. "I, I was just looking for a pen and a piece of paper. I sometimes journal and had forgotten my notebook in my car," he stammered.

I nodded and rose to cross the room to him. "Well, I'm sure you won't find one in the registration book, and there is a pen sitting right there. You actually moved it when you picked up the book to flip through it." I waited for his response, and he just looked at me, studying me. I returned his gaze with one eyebrow raised.

"I had a friend that stayed here about a few months ago." He paused. I waited for him to continue. "His name was Charlie Stone."

"Are you sure it was here? I don't recall a guest by that name." I observed him.

"Yes, I'm sure. He sent me a text with the view from the room… the same room I'm staying in."

"I don't think so. We just finished renovating that room. Only a couple of people have stayed in there since it was done. One was a single young gal, and the other was a couple. Now you. I think you must be mistaken about where he was staying."

He shook his head. "I'm not. Can you show me the register from the end of summer, early fall?"

"I shouldn't, as it is an invasion of privacy for my other guests, but because you are so adamant, I'm happy to show you." I took a key from around my neck and went to the filing cabinet behind the desk. I unlocked the top drawer and pulled out the register book from that time. I handed it to him.

He took it and started flipping through pages. When he got to the end, his finger ran down the list of names. "This was the date he was here."

"Was he actually here?" I asked, looking over his shoulder.

He sighed. "I don't see his name. Would there be another book?"

"No. Unfortunately, we don't get that many guests, as by just looking around, you see you're the only one here."

He handed the book back to me. "Maybe I was mistaken. I'm sorry."

"You could have just asked when you arrived, instead of waiting to sneak out here in the middle of the night like a thief snooping around." I couldn't keep the irritation out of my voice.

"I'm sorry. I shouldn't have." The words sounded sincere, but the shrug of his shoulders gave a different message.

"Why do you think your friend was here?"

"Charlie went for a hike on the Shoreline Greenway Trail last year. He sent me a text with the picture and told me about this place."

I rolled my eyes. "Or you assumed this place. We just proved he didn't stay here."

Thomas's eyes met mine, and I saw the doubt in them. "So, you say."

I laughed. "You saw the registry book. He's not listed in there."

"That doesn't mean a thing." He shot back.

"Were there other names after the day he *supposedly* was here?"

He scowled. "Yes, but…"

"But what?" I was mad now. "What exactly are you accusing me of?"

"I'm not accusing you of anything, but he has been missing for months. The trail has been searched, and there's no trace of him."

"Look, I understand your concern, but you can't just come in here and start throwing out accusations or start snooping around."

"Yeah, I know. I'm frustrated. I feel like the police have given up. It's just, he was like a brother to me."

I nodded. "I get it, but truly rethink your tactics here."

"I am sorry." He turned back toward his room. "I'll be heading out early tomorrow."

I watched him go back to his room. He was almost to his door when I called out, "How about a drink to take the edge off?"

He turned and looked at me. "Whatcha got?"

"I can make you some warm milk, a shot of whiskey... what's your preference?"

"Well, those are two complete opposite choices. As must as I would like the whiskey, I'll take some warm milk."

"Sure. Give me just a couple of minutes."

He moved toward the couch in the living room. "Mind if I wait here?"

I smiled. "Not at all. You can browse the books if you like, but please stop snooping."

I went to the kitchen and started warming the milk. I pulled a mug from the shelf and put in a few drops of my special ingredient. Once the milk was warm, I added it to the cup and started to the living room. He was sitting on the couch. He had a travel book next to him on the sofa, though his head was leaned back with his eyes closed.

I softly cleared my throat to let him know I was back. "Here you go."

He opened his eyes and slowly stood up. "Thanks. I really appreciate it." He started back to his room, mug in hand. He turned at his door. "And I am sorry for snooping."

I nodded. "Good night."

I sat down and waited to give him another thirty minutes before I paid him a visit. My mind wandered to his features. His hair kept coming to mind. Thick, dark hair, with a wave to it. I could have the perfect hair for my man. I smiled and glanced at my watch. It was time. I stood and moved to the bedroom.

I opened the door slowly and let my eyes adjust to the darkness. Thomas was lying in bed. I noticed the mug on the bedside table, half empty. I prayed it had done the trick and walked over to the bed. I carried with me my small box of fishhooks. I had chosen one with a green feather this time.

Thomas was sleeping quite peacefully. I stood there and watched for a few minutes before he seemed to sense someone next to him. His eyes flew open, and he tried to move. Realizing he couldn't, his eyes filled with fear as he stared at me. I leaned close to him. "You're more frightened than Charlie was."

The recognition showed in his eyes at the words. His poor friend, Charlie. I watched him for a moment, just taking in the fear radiating off him. Yes, his hair *was* perfect. Was there another part of him I could keep? I smiled down at him. "Charlie had beautiful blue eyes. Did you know he told me there were plenty of fish in the sea? Once he said that, I just had to have him." I opened the box and took out the fishhook. "I hooked him good, but unfortunately, he then had to sleep with the fishes."

I put the fishhook back in the box and put the box on the side table. "You won't be needing that, though. The only reason you're here now is that you snooped around looking for Charlie. If only you had just left it alone. However, I will send your friend a text from your phone, telling them you found nothing, and that you heard of someone he was seen getting in a car with. That will be the end of you and Charlie."

One of his fingers twitched, and I realized he hadn't drunk enough of the warm milk. It was a good thing I had waited no longer. I blew him a kiss as I reached for the release button behind the headboard and pushed it. His hand shot up as he started to fall, but he wasn't quick enough to grab me. He fell onto the spikes with a scream.

I stood at the top of the pit, looking down at him. He'd been moving when he fell, so he hadn't landed squarely on the bed of spikes. He was definitely still alive and trying desperately to get off a couple of the impaling blades. Between screams of pain and cursing at me, he struggled. I watched him, and finally, he realized it was futile to keep struggling. He was impaled and impaled he would stay. At least the spike had missed the head. I could keep his perfect thick head of hair. It would look good with Charlie's blue eyes.

I pulled the trap door open and went down into the pit. He was still alive, tears pouring from his eyes. Blood ran down the spikes and pooled on the floor. I walked around him, reviewing the damage that had been done. The spikes that had impaled him were significantly placed to ensure his death. I would allow the suffering. After all, I spared him the pain of the fishhook in his cheek.

I slowly lowered the spikes into the ground, and he screamed in pain again as the tips tore from his body. I squatted next to him. He barely moved at this point. "Damn bitch. Why?"

"Oh, Thomas, please don't speak like that. You know why this happened…you stuck your nose in where it shouldn't have been." I brushed my fingers through his hair. It was thick, and yet so soft.

I stood and went to my table, where I found my

scalpel. I tested the sharpness and went back over to Thomas. "It will only hurt for a moment." I skillfully made a slow cut into the end of his face, along the hairline, and patiently cut through the skin, peeling it back until I held his beautiful hair and scalp in my hand. I looked down, and he had passed out from the pain. I put two fingers on his neck. His pulse was weak.

I stood up and returned the scalpel to the table. I pushed the button for the spikes to rise in a quick motion, and the bed of spikes impaled Thomas once again. This time one went through his neck and the blood gurgled around it. I lowered the spiked bed once again and he was free. Dead, but free from the restricting blades.

I wrapped him in plastic, but his scalp took more of my attention. I carefully prepped it and put it in the closet on a wig stand next to the jar of blue eyes. I looked to the picture hanging on the back of the closet door. Charlie's name was in each of the eyes of the drawing of the man. Before I shut the door, I carefully wrote *Thomas* on the scalp.

six

Dawson had spent another sleepless night. The past couple of nights, Ali had been working late and therefore had just stayed at her place. It had been part of the unspoken agreement between them, but damn, he was finding he slept better with her by his side.

It had been a week since they had found the body on the edge of the water. With his dental records, Ali was able to identify him as Charlie Stone.

Dawson headed to the Stones' home. When he arrived, it looked like no one was there, but he went to the front door and rang the doorbell. As he waited a few minutes, the neighbor to the right came out on their porch.

"Are you looking for the Stones?" she called.

"Yes, ma'am. Are they around?" Dawson walked down the front steps and across the lawn to meet the neighbor. "Detective Dawson, ma'am." He held out his business card to her.

"I'm Cheryl. They went out of the country last week. Supposed to be gone for a month. I told them I would keep an eye on the place."

Dawson smiled. This was the type of neighbor he liked to talk with. One who knew everything going on and loved to be in the midst of things and had no problem sharing information. "Did you know Charlie Stone?" he asked.

"Yes, the son. He's been missing for months now. He had a couple of close friends that didn't live far from here. Thomas Levesque and David Nielson. I don't know their exact address, but they lived close enough that they walked here when they were together."

"Thank you, ma'am. That's very helpful. I'll see if I can find them and talk to them. If you think of anything else, please don't hesitate to call me."

"Is that the body you found, Charlie Stone?" she asked.

"I'm not at liberty to reveal that information as of yet. But please, let me know if you think of anything else that might be helpful." Dawson made it clear that the conversation was done as he walked back to his car.

He sat in his car and did a Google search for Thomas Levesque and David Nielson. A David Nielson came up as living just two streets over. Dawson decided that was his next stop. When he drove up in front of the Nielson house, there was a young man sitting on the front steps, smoking a cigarette. Dawson got out and walked up to him.

"I'm looking for a David Nielson." Dawson handed him a business card.

"Cop, huh? I'm David. What can I do for you?"

"Do you know a Charlie Stone?" Dawson asked.

"I did. He's been missing about six months now. Cops didn't seem to care much to find him." He looked down at the card Dawson had handed him. "Not from the East Haven police. They were the ones his disappearance was reported to. They didn't seem to do too much."

"And he just disappeared one day?"

"He went for a hike on the Shoreline Greenway Trail. Sent Tommy a pic of this cool view, then we never heard from him again. He was supposed to have been back the next day."

"Who's Tommy?"

David gestured to the stairs. "Have a seat."

Dawson sat down next to him and waited for him to continue.

"Tommy Levesque. The three of us were best friends. Tommy decided he was going to go looking for him about two months ago."

"Did Tommy find him?" Dawson asked.

"I don't know. I talked to him on the phone. He said he was staying at the last place Charlie had been and would look for something to prove Charlie had been there. I told him not to do anything stupid. The next morning, I got a text from him saying he had talked to someone that had seen Charlie get in a car with someone. The text said he was going to follow that lead. That was the last I heard from him. I tried calling him, but it went right to voice mail.

That was two months ago, and I've heard nothing since. The police found no leads, nothing."

Dawson frowned. "So, Charlie went missing six months ago, and then Tommy went missing two months ago, and no one made the connection?"

"Yup. Reported it to the New Haven Police and again, not much investigation seemed to happen. The police said there was a connection, but they could find no evidence of foul play. I guess it got put on the back burner for them. Their response was *these things happen all the time*. Young guys must have just taken off to go somewhere new and have been too busy to get in touch." David shrugged. "Police don't care. Charlie's parents were devastated. They were really close. After a year, they finally went on a getaway. I wouldn't be surprised if they moved. Too many memories here for them."

"And Tommy? Was he close with his family?" Dawson asked.

"Naw. I can see Tommy taking off, but he would have at least been in touch with me. I was the closest thing he had to family."

Dawson nodded. "Thank you for your time."

Driving to the Branford Police Station, Dawson couldn't help but think there had to be a connection. Both men had been from New Haven, but they were in Madison when they were last heard from. Branford was right in the middle of them. Was it possible that Charlie got in a car with someone and wound up in some trouble? But then, what happened to Thomas?

Dawson sighed. He'd known all along that this

was going to be something more than a seemingly fishing accident.

When he arrived at the station, he went straight to the conference room where his victimology board had been set up. Right now, Charlie was the lone picture up on it with very little written next to it. Dawson wrote in all caps on a piece of paper THOMAS and pinned it next to Charlie's picture. He pulled out his cell phone and punched in the numbers to the State Police Headquarters.

"Kathy speaking."

Dawson smiled. His favorite person in the department, or at least he kept telling her that. She was the magic one who could dig up anything someone was looking for… if it was to be found at all. "Kathy, how's it going?"

"Dawson. Lord, I thought you'd fallen off the face of the earth. We never get to see your face around here anymore."

"Trust me, there are times I would much rather be there than out here working on these cases."

Kathy's laughter faded. "Got yourself another serial killer?"

"I'm not sure yet. But I could use your help if you have a few minutes to spare me."

"Anything for you. Whatcha need?"

Dawson smiled and pulled his notebook out. "I have two friends that went missing. A Charles Stone and a Thomas Levesque. Charles was six months ago and Thomas, two months ago. Both last seen in Madison at some inn. Not sure of the name. All I know is it's near the Shoreline Greenway Trail."

"So, you need some background information on the inn for that time frame?"

"Yes, please," Dawson poured on the charm. "I will owe you big time."

"Honey, if I kept score of every time you told me you owed me, you would be one poor man. Give me a little bit and I'll call you back." Her laughter was cut off as she disconnected the call.

Not ten minutes went by when his cell phone rang. "Dawson."

"Got the names you wanted. There are three inns in that area—*Lifeline Inn, Sailor's Bluff, and Oceanview*. It looks likes *Oceanview* is closed, but the other two have been open a number of years. I'll try and track down who owned that one and *Sailor's Bluff*. The *Lifeline Inn* is owned by Phelps Enterprises. Not much information about that company. I can do some more digging, but it will take a while."

"That was quick. Thanks so much, Kathy."

She was gone without a word. Dawson pulled his laptop closer and did a quick Google search for the Phelps Enterprises. As Kathy said, there wasn't much information available for the company. Dawson decided he may need to pay a visit to the Madison Police Department to get more information regarding the situation.

Ali continued to contemplate the body in locker twenty. The fishhook in the mouth seemed almost like a signature, but while researching, she couldn't come up with any known suspects that used a fishing hook as an MO. She sat back in her chair and stared at the computer. Her gut told her there was more to this story than what they were seeing.

Another ghost?

She leaned forward and reached for the keyboard again. She searched past killers in Google who killed with a fishing hook. Nothing. She sighed. She was missing something, but she couldn't put her finger on what it was… and it was driving her crazy.

Lately, she and Dawson were like two ships passing in the night. This new case had him out of town, and between the late nights with her at work and his traveling back and forth, they hadn't seen each other much. She missed him. Not just the talking and his company, but his touch.

Ali went back to the morgue and pulled out locker twenty. She studied the holes that had gone through his body. They weren't huge puncture holes, but they were large enough to be significant in size and enough to kill him. She measured the wounds themselves, and then the distance between them. She grabbed a piece of paper and drew a diagram of the layout. The holes corresponded to a straight line, with the bottom ones being one in each of his thighs. Obviously, strategically placed.

She went back to her computer and did another search for death by impalement. There were a few interesting results. When she glanced at her watch, she realized she was late for a meeting and would have to revisit this later and discuss it with Wes. Hopefully, she would see him tonight.

seven

Dawson stared down at his laptop. He was sitting in the Branford Police Station in his makeshift office. He started pulling missing person reports from the surrounding areas. Charlie and Thomas came up, as well as a handful of others that all seemed to have been marked as cold cases. Most of them were men, all in their twenties and single. They all seemed to fit an initial profile that could be what their killer was looking for.

Dawson took a break when he had a list of a dozen young men. He would start with those names and go from there. Most of them were from the New Haven area, so one stop at that police department should give him a good indication if they were all in the same category or if they were just random, missing men.

Before he headed to New Haven, Dawson also pulled up the Shoreline Greenway Trail. It was a hiking trail from East Haven to Madison. Typically, about an eight-hour hike one way. He pulled up a map and searched for inns or hotels along the way. There were a bunch in New Haven and at the Madison end of the trail, and there were three inns—or bed-and-breakfast places—that Kathy had told him about. With a plan put together of what to tackle first, Dawson headed for the door.

He stopped by Captain Harris's office first, letting him know he was going to be gone at least the rest of the day and what he was looking for. Harris agreed and told him to let him know if any of his men could help him out.

Dawson took the time in the car to drive to New Haven to think through his plan. First stop was the police department. He had six names on his list that had been reported to the New Haven Police Department as missing. They didn't all have the same investigating officer, but at least if he could speak with the Chief of Police there, he might get some initial answers. He had a feeling this was going to be tedious work that wouldn't yield any results immediately. He pulled into the parking lot of the police station, which was busy. New Haven was a good-size city and noted for having a large amount of crime activity, so it did not surprise him by the busyness of the station.

He entered. Once he finally got up to the clerk on duty, he flashed his badge and asked to speak with the captain. He was directed to the office, and he knocked on the door.

"Enter," a voice called.

Dawson pushed open the door. "Sir, Detective Wes Dawson from the State Police."

The man behind the desk rose. "Captain Benton Grayson. What can I do for you?" He held out his hand to shake Dawson's. "Sit down."

Dawson sank into the chair. "Sir, I'm looking into some missing person reports that have come up as cold cases. I've got a homicide victim who appears to be on my list of missing persons and wanted to check on the other names to see where the investigation ended for these men."

Grayson sat back in his chair. "Well, if it ended as a cold case, there must have been no more evidence to find."

Dawson nodded. "I'm not here looking to see if any mistakes were made. I deal with serial killers, sir, and I want to make sure whether or not this victim is leading me into another serial killer hunt."

Grayson nodded. "I heard about your last case. The girl with the hatchet... Lizzie Borden, was it?" He chuckled.

"Unfortunately, yes." Dawson smirked. He was getting sick of the jokes surrounding the hatchet case and didn't want to be looking at another copy-cat of another past killer.

"Well, let's see the list." Dawson placed it on the desk in front of Grayson. He looked down the list and at the officers' names that had been working on them. "Couple of these men are on duty today. Let me see if they are available to talk to you."

Dawson nodded as the chief picked up his phone

and made a call. Upon someone answering, the chief spoke direct. "Get in here." He hung up the phone without another word. Dawson knew this was going to be an uphill battle if the captain already felt like Dawson was second-guessing their investigations. He wasn't, but apparently someone was a bit sensitive about it. Maybe there was a reason for that. He had already heard how David had felt his friends' disappearance was brushed off—that no one cared about Tommy or Charlie. Time would tell.

A young man stepped into the office. The captain and Dawson stood up. "Wallace, this is Detective Dawson from the State Police. Wants to ask you some questions about your missing person reports from a few months back."

Wallace held out his hand to shake Dawson's. "Nice to meet you, Detective."

"Please, call me Dawson. Mind if we talk a bit?" Dawson gestured toward the door, hoping that if the captain wasn't listening, this young cop would be more forthcoming about his investigation.

"Sure. Come out to my desk and I can pull any files you might need." Wallace led the way out to the bull pen and Dawson sat in the chair next to the desk where the young man sat. "I assume you're looking at specific missing people?"

"Yes." Dawson had grabbed the list from the captain's desk, and he placed it in front of the young man. "This first one on the list, Charlie Stone, was just found dead. I deal with serial killers and am looking into the possibility of some of the other men on this list finding the same fate Mr. Stone did."

The man sat back. "I remember that case. It was the first one I worked on here. There wasn't much to go on, and then a few months later we got a report that one of his friends was missing as well. The case was cold from Stone, and so when Levesque was reported missing, I'll admit I did a little bit of investigating, talked to some neighbors and friends, but that's as far as it went."

"You never looked into the last place they'd been. One of their friends said they were both at the same place right before they went missing. Levesque apparently called his other friend and told him he was where Charlie had been the last time they'd talked to him."

Wallace slowly shook his head. "No, I don't recall ever having that information." He turned toward his computer and pulled up the files on Thomas Levesque and Charlie Stone. He printed them out and handed them to Dawson. As Dawson skimmed through them, both files were very thin on details. No mention of a hotel or inn that they had been at, nor mention of the hike that supposedly they had gone on from New Haven to Madison.

"What about any of the other names on the list? A few of them were from this area also." Dawson wasn't impressed so far with what they had in the files on the first two.

"I didn't handle those, but I can bring up the files." He brought up another three missing men on the computer, and the files had even less information in them. "I'm afraid this isn't going to help you much." The young man shrugged.

"Is this typical of missing persons?" Dawson tried to keep the irritation out of his voice.

"We have a lot of runaways around here, so yeah, missing persons get marked as cold cases pretty quickly unless there is some real hard and fast evidence."

Dawson nodded. "Thanks for your time." He stood and headed back to the front door. He poked his head into the captain's office on his way out. "Thanks for letting me talk with your man, Grayson. I appreciate the help."

"I hope it was useful." Grayson gave a brief nod, dismissing Dawson.

eight

With the abrupt change in temperature as the winter season came rolling in, suddenly the inn was busy as it ever had been for this time of year. I was thrilled. There'd been a slow period where the owners had talked about closing it, but they hung in there and now it was thriving again. I liked to think I had something to do with it, but it was mainly because of most tourists coming around and needing a place to stay. Being close to Christmas, it was unusual to be at capacity, but apparently, the new thing to do was travel for the holidays.

I was setting up for the cocktail hour in the living room. All the rooms upstairs were full and Room 1, the lone room on the first floor, had a single, young, good-looking man in it. When he came in, I had noticed immediately the flawless skin on his face.

Most girls would die for blemish-free skin like that. I looked forward to maybe having a conversation with him this evening with *drinks,* and I smiled inwardly at the pleasant thought.

He'd been another hiker on the Shoreline Greenway Trail, which was always perfect as they didn't have a car with them and rarely could be traced back to having stayed at this inn. Of course, I had perfected my abilities at forging signatures in case I needed to rework a page in the registry. The owners had talked about doing away with the registration books and wanted to move to digital records. I had convinced them, for the time being, that the old-fashioned way was one quirk of the inn that people loved. I knew that wouldn't last forever, and hopefully, I could figure out how to forge or permanently delete digital reservations.

Darren walked into the living room and pulled me from my thoughts. Darren Weldon. A rugged man, not all that tall, but height didn't matter for what I had in mind for him.

"Am I the first one here?" Darren asked.

"You are, but someone has to be. What's your pleasure tonight? We have a red wine, white wine, or a Vodka Martini is the special cocktail tonight."

He grinned. "I'll go with the Vodka Martini. Maybe it'll bring out my inner James Bond."

I smiled as I went to the small bar that had been set up. Ramsay was making the cocktails tonight, and he whipped it together. As I handed it to Darren, other guests started coming downstairs. This cocktail hour and hors d'oeuvres had become quite popular here at the inn and Ramsay was constantly creating something new to serve to the guests. We always had wine and provided one specialty cocktail to choose from. Ramsay and I enjoyed it, but Minnie stayed in her room, claiming she hated the interaction, which was why she enjoyed being the housekeeper.

After everyone was served and mingling around, I joined Darren off to the side. He was our only single there tonight, and I hated to see him standing alone. "Enjoying yourself?"

"I am. This is a great way to unwind after the hike today. I'll sleep like a baby tonight."

"Did you make reservations for dinner somewhere this evening?"

He shook his head. "I decided I was just going to order a small pizza to be delivered here to eat in my room. I love the view, and thought I'd just kick back and relax to enjoy it."

"You definitely can't beat the view." I acknowledged. "Excuse me, as I check in with other guests."

"I don't want to monopolize your time."

I watched him off and on while I mingled with the others and made my way back around the room toward him. He had moved over to the bar to talk to Ramsay. As the guests started dispersing to the various dinner plans, Ramsay and I began cleaning up the living room from various glassware.

Ramsay went into the kitchen, and Darren approached me. "Did you have plans for dinner?"

I shook my head. "I typically grab something from the kitchen while the guests are out with their dinner plans. I'll be around here until everyone is in bed."

He watched me. "Would like to share a pizza? We could sit out on the deck and enjoy the view together, if it's not too cold for you."

I smiled. "I'd enjoy that."

"Great. I'll call in the pizza order, and I'll meet you on the deck when it gets here?"

I nodded. "I'll bring the beers."

I was waiting on the deck with two beers on the table with some paper plates and napkins when Darren showed up carrying a pizza box. "I didn't think to ask what you liked, so I went with the standard of pepperoni."

"That's fine." I put out the plates and napkins as Darren sat down. We both reached in and ate in silence. When we had our fill, we moved the chairs to the railing of the deck to sit and enjoy the moon sparkling on the water. "Did you hike the trail alone?"

"Yeah. It was a goal of mine a year ago when I first moved to the New Haven area. It just took me a while to get it done."

"Where did you move from?" I took a sip of beer.

"Decided to try the east coast after living in California for a decade. Needed a change of scenery."

I nodded silently, waiting for him to continue.

"You ever have a time in your life where you just need a change of scenery, a chance to really just start over?"

"Definitely." I frowned. "Sometimes it works out, and sometimes it doesn't."

"Sounds like there's a story there. And since I've been doing most of the talking, fill me in on this story." Darren looked over at me.

"Not much to tell. I'm really not that interesting of a person. My life is boring."

Darren scoffed. "Come on. I don't believe that for a second."

I smiled. "Well, I was engaged a few years back, and it didn't work out. So, I wandered about for a little while, visiting different states, and ended up here. I couldn't resist this place, next to the water, and then when I landed this job, it just seemed like it was destiny for me to be here."

"Well, I guess you got the better deal after the breakup." Darren spoke softly.

I glanced over and smiled. "Thank you. I think so, too."

"Besides, you know there are always more fish in the sea... no pun intended." He chuckled.

I froze. Not again. Why do the good ones always screw it up? I knew this would be the last evening he would see, so I sat in silence. After watching the moon glimmer off the waves for a while, I stood. "I really need to finish up some things. Thanks for the pizza and the company."

Darren nodded. "Thank you. I really enjoyed it."

"Can I get you anything else? Another drink?"

"I'll take another beer, if that is a possibility."

I nodded. "I'll grab that for you." I left for the kitchen and glanced back at Darren still sitting in the chair next to the railing. "It didn't have to be this way," I softly whispered.

As I opened a beer for him, I glanced around the kitchen. Ramsay and Minnie had already cleaned up and gone to their rooms. The clock on the stove read ten-twenty p.m. It was late enough, and hopefully, he would just go to bed. I put a few drops of the elixir in his beer and started back out with it.

When I got to the deck, Darren was standing by the railing, and he turned to face me. "I just realized the time. I'm sorry I kept you from your duties for so long."

I handed him the beer. "Don't worry. I'm a bit of a night owl, so I can easily finish up what I need to. Thanks again for the pizza."

He nodded. I had the feeling if I gave him any encouragement, he'd lean forward and kiss me, so I took a step back. "Have a good night." I turned and headed to the desk to at least look busy while Darren proceeded to his room and shut the door.

I sighed as I sat down at the desk and pulled the registry towards me. This one could be tricky, since he had interacted with everyone tonight at the cocktail hour. Luckily, most of our guests were out of state and hopefully, would never return here… or at least not for a long time. By then, they would have forgotten the fair-skinned man who broke my heart.

After fifteen minutes had passed, I grabbed my small box from the locked drawer in the desk and started toward Room 1. I turned the knob and realized he had locked it. *Damn it.*

I retraced my steps to the desk and got out the master key. Back at the door, I gently unlocked it and opened it. I stepped into the dark room and quietly shut the door behind me. I could make out Darren lying in bed from the moonlight coming through the partially closed binds, as well as the beer bottle on the nightstand. I picked it up and shook it, near empty. I smiled.

"Darren," I whispered.

I flipped on the small reading lamp on the nightstand. His eyes opened, and I gleefully watched as the realization struck that he couldn't move or talk. He searched my face; questions filled his eyes with a hint of fear.

"I really enjoyed our time tonight," I said, flirty. "I just wish you hadn't talked about the fish in the sea. My fiancé broke up with me because there were better fish in the sea to go after. I never truly recovered from it." A sharp pain struck behind my eyes again. A voice in my head said, *he's the mark. Do it now.* I couldn't place the voice, but it was authoritative, and I nodded. I pulled out the fishhook from the box I had carried. "A nice green feather for you, but this will have to wait until the next step."

I leaned over him and ran my fingers along his jaw. "I don't want to mar this pretty face quite yet. I had such high hopes for you."

I reached for the button behind the headboard and dropped the bed. The lights on the motion sensor flicked on, and he hit the bed of spikes.

Thunk!

The sickening sound resonated as all five spikes hit their mark. At least he had a quick death.

I pushed the button to pull the bed back into place and straightened the covers, then moved to the closet. I opened the trap door and headed down to my trophy room. When I entered the room, I knew he was gone. I lowered the spikes. Once they retracted from Darren and he lay peacefully on the floor, I gently washed his face with a wet cloth. Lovingly, I made sure there was no blood on his perfect skin, and then prepared it for harvesting with the cleaning solution. Removing facial skin was more time consuming than the extractions I'd done before, but Darren's handsome face was worth the effort. Once it was complete, with the facial skin fully intact, I immediately placed it in saline and put it in the refrigerator. I picked up the fishhook and hooked Darren's skinless cheek.

I opened the closet to label my diagram with Darren's name and started preparing his body to dump. A sharp pain hit me directly above my right eye. The strength of the pain dropped me to my knees, and I held my head, praying it would stop. I gritted my teeth. The relentless agony lasted for a few minutes before the flashes of images started: a room barely furnished, except for the bed and chair. No curtains on the windows.

Where was that?

Why this one? A voice I didn't recognize screamed in my head. *You know why.* A male voice responded. I shook my head, trying to get their conversation to stop. They seemed so familiar, yet complete strangers. Although it felt as if I'd been on my knees holding my head for an hour, in reality, only a few minutes had passed. After the pain faded and I could stand, I rushed to get Darren taken care of. I didn't need Ramsay or Minnie waking up and looking for me.

nine

It was time to go in a different direction. Dawson pulled the loaner laptop the station had let him use, so he wouldn't have to lug his around, and plugged in Phelps Enterprises. It was an international holding company with multiple real estate holdings. Most were small inns or hotels, while others were resorts.

Just as Kathy had said, the company's owners were listed as an LLC with no names attached to them. He hated this type of research. It was a long process, and he had hoped Kathy had dug up more, but he couldn't fault her. She was good at what she did. He tried a different tactic. He did a search for all inns located in Madison. There were only the three that Kathy had given him—and not far from each other—all on the coast.

Dawson jumped in the car and headed toward Leighton. His stomach had settled a bit by the time he parked his car in front of the medical examiner's office. The sterile smell assaulted him as he walked down the hall to Ali's office. He found her hiding behind a stack of folders on her desk, typing away at the computer.

"Hey, anything new?" Dawson leaned against the doorframe.

"Well, hello. This is a surprise. It's been a while since you showed up at my office. Need a phone charger?" She grinned.

Dawson smiled at her reference of the first conversation they'd had while he was borrowing her phone charger. "Believe it or not, I actually remember to charge my phone these days."

"I don't believe it. I imagine you have a girlfriend who reminds you."

Dawson shook his head. "Always taking the credit."

"How are you feeling?" Ali's voice softened with concern.

"I'm good. Frustrated with this case, but good." He cleared her chair of files and sat down. "I think I'm going to head to Madison and poke around three inns that are out there to see if anyone recognizes Charlie or his friend Thomas, who is also on the missing person's list."

"Keep me posted on what you find out, but be careful."

Dawson smirked. "Aren't I always?"

She shrugged. "Not really, but that's another conversation."

He laid his head back against the wall and closed his eyes for a moment. "We need a vacation. When this case is over, why don't we go away for a few days?"

"We might be able to do that. However, just because your case ends doesn't mean my work is done, too. I don't just do autopsies exclusively on your cases."

"Yeah, well, you should." Dawson stood and leaned over to capture her lips with his. The kiss was soft and slow. He pulled back just a hair and whispered, "I've missed you."

"I'll see you tonight." Ali gave him another kiss before pushing him toward the door. "*If* I can get my work done."

Dawson drove with the window down as he headed up the coastal route toward Madison. His mind wandered to his sister, Sara. She had been elusive for the past few years, leaving notes here and there for him, telling him to stop searching for her. But he refused to quit looking. He wanted, *needed*, to find her. It frustrated him to no end to be worried about her constantly and her being so blasé about encountering him. They used to be close. How could she possibly think he would just let her go and live on the street and be okay with that?

Dawson pulled into the parking lot of the first inn he came to: *Sailor's Bluff*. It was a small rustic place that had recently been painted. The roof looked new and made him wonder how long it had actually been running as an inn.

He rang the doorbell and waited. The door opened and a young girl, probably no more than seventeen or eighteen, stood before him.

"Hi, can I help you?"

"Detective Wes Dawson." He flashed his badge. "Is the owner around?"

The girl nodded. "Come on in. Mom's in the kitchen." She stood back and closed the door after Dawson entered the house.

He glanced around. It had a spacious living room with a small desk to the side. A hallway continued to the right, which showed three closed doors that he assumed to be rooms. The girl had disappeared to get the mother, so Dawson took a couple of steps farther toward the hallway and looked to the left. The girl and her mother approached from what he assumed to be the kitchen.

"Detective Dawson, was it?" The woman held her hand. "I'm Maria Olssen. How can I help you?"

Dawson shook her hand. "Pleased to meet you. I'm just trying to gather some information. How long have you been in business here?"

Maria gestured to the couch in the living room. She waited until Dawson sat down. "I opened three years ago. Previously, it was an old house that my grandfather left to me, and it took me a couple of years to get it renovated so we could open."

Dawson nodded. "Do you have a lot of guests?"

"The inn has three bedrooms on this floor, which I use for guests. Kylie and I sleep upstairs in our private rooms. It stays fairly full in the summertime and into early fall. We pretty much are empty through the winter months, and then it picks up again sporadically in spring." She paused. "Has something happened I should know about?"

Dawson smiled. "I'm helping with a missing person, and he was in this area about six months ago. Would you have had a young man by the name of Charlie Stone staying here about that time frame?"

"That name doesn't ring a bell, but let me check my records." She went over to the small desk near the front door and pulled out a registration book. She flipped back a few pages and scrolled down the names. "I don't see anyone with that name from the past six to eight months."

"I appreciate your help." He stood and shook her hand again.

Before he got back on the road, Dawson sat in his car and crossed *Sailor's Bluff* off his list. Two more to go. How hard could it be to find a place where both Charlie and Thomas stayed? He turned back onto the coastal road to head toward the next one listed: the *Lifeline Inn*. Since the third on the list was closed and likely a dead end, this one was the most probable. It wasn't far, and Dawson wondered how some of these inns could survive at all, being so close to each other. He turned into the parking lot and sat in his car a moment, taking in the view.

The two-story, old Victorian house seemed to be in good shape, but definitely not as new as the last one. There were flower beds on each side of the front door filled with blossoming plants. Dawson got out of the car and glanced around. He was parked to the side of the house, and he stood looking out over the ocean. The view was definitely gorgeous, and he could see the appeal to staying there.

He went to the front door and knocked, and a young man opened the door. Tattoos peeked out from his shirt sleeves that were rolled up to his elbows.

Dawson flashed his badge. "Detective Wes Dawson."

"Come in. What can I do for you?" The man stood back for Dawson to enter.

"You are?"

"Jake Clement."

"Are you the owner, sir?"

The man gave a small chuckle. "Not hardly. I'm just the cook and jack-of-all-trades to do some small handyman things. Owners aren't around."

Dawson nodded. "How long has this inn been running?"

The man shrugged. "Don't know exactly. I've been working here about four years. It had been an inn prior, then the present owners bought it about six years ago."

"Did they run it personally at that time?"

The man scowled. "I really don't know. Is there something specific you're needing to know?"

Dawson smiled pleasantly. "Contact information of the owners, if possible."

The man walked to a desk against the wall and grabbed a business card. *Lifeline Inn, proprietors Ronald and Marisa Connors* with the number at the inn. Were they the names behind Phelps Enterprises? "Do you have a personal number where I could reach them?"

The man sighed and went to the rolodex on the desk. He riffled through it and stopped, then scribbled a number on a piece of paper and handed it to him. "Here you go."

Dawson grabbed it and glanced down at the number. It was an international number. "Thank you."

The man grunted and stood there, waiting for Dawson to leave. Obviously, he wasn't a fan of the police. Dawson pocketed the card and paper with the number on it. "Is there a manager that runs the place while the owners are away?"

Jake shrugged. "Olivia. She's not in right now."

Dawson nodded. "I'm looking for a couple of men that might have stayed here. Can I at least take a look at the records to see if they were here?"

Jake sneered. "Even *I* know that isn't legal. Buddy, Olivia couldn't let you see them either. Your best bet is to get ahold of the owners, or get a warrant."

Dawson smiled and nodded "Thanks for your help."

He glanced back at the house as he made his way to his car.

The ride to the third inn, *Oceanview*, was uneventful and a complete waste of time. Kathy had said the place was closed, but as soon as Dawson drove up to it, he assumed it had been abandoned *years* ago. It had broken windows, peeling paint, and grass growing in the gravel driveway.

Despite the obvious abandonment, Dawson parked the car, walked around the property, and tried to peer in the filth-laden windows. There was nothing too obvious, but one could never know for sure. Maybe this was just the place his killer was holed up in. He tried the doors, but they were locked. He made a mental note to look for leads on who owned this property, so he could get permission to search it.

Well, he at least had the contact information for one of the inn's owners to contact. If that was a bust, he was out of leads *and* ideas.

ten

The inn continued to do well, and lately, I felt content in life. The headaches and flashes of memories— if you could call them that—had settled down. No men had come to the inn talking about *fish in the sea*, and therefore, my revenge need had subsided. It was the week of Christmas, and I was glad for the break.

The owners had gone digital, and I was learning the system. The process that allowed guests to book their room and pay via credit card online was going smoothly, and I was learning the ins and outs of reversing charges, if necessary, upon cancellations. Even how to initiate the cancellation on my end. All reasonable research for when the time came that another fish-in-the-sea pompous male walked through the door. *Damn trolls.*

I scrolled through the reservations, seeing who was left to check in today. Room 1 was booked with a single man. Kevin O'Neil. *Hmm, this ought to be interesting.* The bed had not been released from its moors in over several months. Although I'd been glad for the reprieve, there was a faint niggling in my mind, telling me I needed the kill. I had to finish my collection for my creation of the perfect man. He still needed a few more parts, and I couldn't keep everything that I had gathered thus far on hold much longer. It was time to finish up.

I had made a fresh batch of my belladonna elixir, and I was ready. My body flushed hotly as the old familiar stabbing pain behind my right eye came again. As usual, with the pain came flashes of images: a bedroom, the spikes, blood. Usually, I heard a faraway laughter, but only in my head. Where was it coming from? I didn't recognize any of those things. It had been a while since they started, but these flash-like memories had grown stronger once I moved into the inn, and after I had found the room.

My rumination was cut short when the door opened and a tall, blond-headed, muscular man walked in the door. He had a flat-top haircut, military style, and moved like he owned the place. "Good evening."

I stood behind the desk and smiled. "Welcome. You must be Kevin."

"Yes, ma'am." He dropped his bag on the floor in front of the desk.

I clicked a few buttons on the computer to pull up his reservation. "We have the Visa on file. Will that be the card you want charged?"

"Yes, please."

"You're in Room 1." I gestured toward the door beyond the stairway. "Right over there."

"Great. Sorry for the late arrival, and I'll be leaving early in the morning."

I nodded. "Is this a business or pleasure trip?" The stabbing pain in my eye came back full force, and it was all I could do not to grab my head in agony.

"Pleasure. Just making my way up the coast." He seemed intentionally vague in his answers, but that wasn't uncommon for people who tried to be private.

"You missed the cocktail hour and hors d'oeuvres, but I am happy to get you something to eat if you're hungry."

He flashed me a smile. "I'm good. Thank you. I'm just going to retire for the night."

I nodded and sat back down as he made his way to the bedroom. This was not going to work well if I couldn't engage him in conversation at all.

He's not the one. The voice rang in my mind, startling me. I glanced around the room and saw no one. Not the one for what? For killing? He was a good-looking man and could fit any number of required parts.

No, not the one.

I was agitated now. Who was talking? And how did they know what I wanted?

I went to the deck and looked out to the water. I allowed myself to go into a half-trance, staring at the water and the gentle waves as they rippled. As I gazed, the half-trance brought to life a reel of pictures in my mind: a man with a black Stetson hat and a scowl on his face. An old room with no furnishings. The outside of a house that could have been the inn centuries ago.

None of it made sense. I tried to focus in on the details, but the pictures were flying by in my mind and didn't allow for focusing in on just one. A door slamming pulled me from my trance-like state, and I turned toward the house.

Kevin was standing on the deck with a sheepish grin on his face. "Sorry about that. I didn't mean to shut the door so hard. I saw the view and wanted to take a closer look."

"No problem. I was lost in my thoughts. Come on out." I turned back toward the railing and peered out over the water again. Goosebumps ran up my spine as a chill came over me. I felt his presence as he moved closer to the railing, although not right next to me. I continued to look at the ocean, ignoring him the best I could.

"This is incredible," he said softly.

"Yes, it is." The instant the words left my lips, the pain hit in my right eye again. Why was this happening so much tonight?

"I'm sorry if I appeared rude back there. I...It's just been a long day."

"No need to apologize. Can I get you anything to help you sleep? Warm milk?"

He grinned. "Is that an old wives' tale that warm milk will help you sleep?"

"It actually does help. I tend to make mine with a bit of vanilla in it with a dash of cinnamon on top." I tried to entice him.

"That sounds good, but I'm not much of a milk drinker. I'm going to head in. Enjoy your night." He turned and went back inside before I could say a thing.

Fool. The word rang in my head, and I couldn't determine if it was me who was the fool or Kevin. I tried to shake off the icy feeling still clinging to me, but the persistent coldness pushed me toward the door. As I went inside, my feet moved me across the living room—making me powerless to stop—and brought me to the bar where a bottle of whiskey sat on top. I pulled down two glasses and put about two fingers in each. I downed one of them and grimaced at the burn in my throat.

I picked up the other glass, put a few drops of belladonna in it, and moved to Room 1. I knocked on the door and waited. Kevin opened it and tilted his head at me in question.

"You don't like milk, but maybe a shot of whiskey will help you sleep." I held out the glass to him.

He smiled but seemed to hesitate before reaching out to take the glass. "Thanks." He gave me a brief nod, and then closed the door. I pressed my ear to it but couldn't hear much. Either he moved extremely quietly, or he was standing on the other side of the door, waiting for me to leave.

I returned to the desk. The niggling feeling told me that even though I had given him the belladonna, I needed to stay away from him. This was not going to end well, and I'd have to forget him as one of my required pieces.

I fought my urge to go to him. The voices in my

head said, *he's not the one. Wait for the right one*. It was hard not to go and see if my special ingredient had worked, but I also had this feeling that he wasn't going to drink it since he'd hesitated taking it from me.

The next morning, I was at the front desk when he came out of the room to check out. "I hope you had a good night."

"Great night sleep, thank you. I just may be back." He smiled and was off.

After he left, I went into his room and found the whiskey glass, untouched. My instinct had been right. He was a very untrusting person.

I grabbed the glass to toss the contents, not wanting Minnie or Ramsay to find it and drink it. That would not be a good thing.

eleven

Sara glanced at the menu. These business dinners were always the worst, but she couldn't complain too much since they usually took place in a nice restaurant and the conversation wasn't always that bad. Her eyes took in the scene around her. This high-scale restaurant was dimly lit with soft music playing in the background. Sara always enjoyed being there.

"What are you having?" she asked.

"Probably the steak. You?" The man never looked up from his menu and sometimes Sara felt that the company wasn't all it could be.

"I think I'll have the lobster." She watched his face for some reaction, but he just nodded. She shook her head, placed the menu at the edge of the table, and continued to watch people as they came in and sat down. People-watching was a favorite pastime of hers, and it never got old trying to figure out who was there for business dinners or dates.

After they ordered, Sara excused herself and headed toward the restroom. She turned the corner and stopped short. A short distance from her, Wes was there with a phone pressed to his ear. He was listening with a scowl on his face, and she smiled. Although he had aged, he still had that boyish charm she had loved in her little brother. That scowl he would turn on her when trying to be mad at her. He never stayed that way long.

The sight of him made her pause. She hadn't been ready to see him like this. She'd been keeping tabs on him and leaving him notes regularly, telling him to stop searching for her, but he would *never* stop. She knew this, but she wasn't ready to face him yet. He'd become a police detective, and she wasn't ready to be happy for him in that capacity.

As he turned his back to her, she scurried to the women's room, her head turned away from him. Although it had been fifteen years since she had left home and ultimately seen Wes face to face, she couldn't take the chance that he would recognize her.

She stared at herself in the restroom mirror. Her dark eyes stared back at her. Wes used to say her eyes were wide with wonder, yet as she looked at herself, all she saw were eyes that held no happiness. Where had the days gone where she was ready for the adventure, wanting more in life? Now, she spent her days living a good, comfortable life, and there was definitely more that she could want for, yet she had lost the desire for adventure.

As she went to return to her seat, she paused to scan ahead of her, searching for Wes. She didn't see him until she turned the corner into the room where her table was. There he stood, next to her table, talking to Douglas, the man she was with that night. She stood still and watched them carefully, ready to flee back to the restroom if need be. Douglas shook his head at something Wes said, and then they shook hands. Wes took his leave and headed toward the front door. Sara managed to turn her head in the other direction before he could see her. She waited until he left the restaurant before returning to her seat.

"Who was that?" she asked when she sat down.

"What?" The man looked up from his phone. "Oh, an old friend. Haven't seen him in years. He recognized me and stopped to say hello."

Sara nodded. An old friend. That was news to her, and she was not happy about it. She sat back and waited for Douglas to continue, but he had returned to his emails and was ignoring her. When the waiter came with their food, Sara held up a hand. "Could you put mine in a box to go, please?"

Douglas looked up in surprise. "Why?"

"I'm not feeling well. I'm just going to take mine to go and head home to rest." The waiter nodded, and after placing Douglas's food in front of him, returned to the kitchen with hers to prepare it for her to take home.

Douglas watched her for a moment, and then just nodded. "Suit yourself. Should I consider our business done then?"

"For tonight." Sara stood as the waiter returned. "We'll talk later."

Sara caught the first cab she could grab and headed for home. Once there, she changed into dark clothing, grabbed her keys, and rushed out the door. She arrived a block from Wes's house in about twenty minutes. She parked and walked down the sidewalk, staying to the shadows. She skirted around the large hedges near Wes's garage and watched his house. She could see him working out with his punching bag and knew he was feeling frustrated. Whether it was the case he was working on, or her, she wasn't sure. She knew she was a source of his frustration, but if he wasn't careful, he would be putting her in jeopardy.

She stayed to the shadows and crept toward his front door, where she left a note under the brick that he kept on his top step. He left it there knowing that was where she would leave her messages. This one was earlier than expected as she had been leaving them every three months. She slowly turned the handle of the door to make sure it wasn't latched. She needed to get his attention. As she backed away, her eyes stayed on the door. She moved back to the garage and threw a small rock at the door, not with much force, but enough to make it bang and get his attention. She stayed behind the hedges and watched as he came to the door.

He immediately bent down and pulled the paper from under the rock. "Sara! Where are you?"

She stayed silent as she kept watching him. He ran his fingers through his hair and closed his eyes. "Why aren't you talking with me?" he said much quieter. "You know I miss you." He moved back into the house and latched the door.

Sara turned and made her way to her car. She always had a twinge of guilt when she left him notes, but she wasn't ready to see him face to face yet. He would be so disappointed in her, and she wanted to let him have the illusion that she was truly okay.

Dawson didn't look at the note until he got to the kitchen. He placed it on the counter and went to the fridge for a beer. He twisted the cap off and took a long drink. This note had come earlier than he expected. Was she in trouble? Did she finally want to meet up? No, of course not, otherwise she would have shown herself.

He knew she was out there watching him, he felt he was being watched every time he got one of her notes. He knew his sister, and she wouldn't leave the note and just go away. She'd stay and make sure he found it. Probably, this was what frustrated him the most, knowing she was within steps of him, and yet, she hid herself.

He took another long drink and set his beer down, then picked up the note.

Wes, if you have ever loved me, you need to stop looking for me. Please think of me and stay away.

He froze. This was the first time she'd written more than she was fine. This seemed like more of a *plea*. Was she in some sort of trouble? His mind whirled with the possibilities of what could be going on, or was this just some game to her? He picked up his phone and snapped a picture of the note. Ali was working late, and they had agreed she was going to stay at her place tonight, but he sent the picture to her anyway.

Just letting you know this came earlier. We'll talk tomorrow.

Without waiting for a reply, he set the phone down and went to jump in the shower.

twelve

Dawson had not slept well. His dreams were filled with murdered bodies, all taking the face of his sister, Sara…her eighteen-year-old face since he hadn't seen her after she left home. He had tossed and turned all night until, finally, at three a.m. he got up and paced around the house. He had arrived at the station by five. He was trying to keep his anger in check, but he was enraged at the note Sara had left him last night. Everyone was steering a wide berth around him today.

He had brought his own travel mug of coffee and shut himself in the conference room, and for the past two hours, he'd been staring at the victimology board. They had one victim with a fishhook in his cheek and eyes removed, but multiple missing men.

Dawson circled the table that he'd been sitting at and stood in front of the pictures of the victim hanging on the board, which was gruesome at best, as well as the picture of his missing friend. He downed the last of his coffee and turned toward his paper on the table. Time to figure out who was behind this before more bodies started piling up.

They had Charlie's body, but hadn't found his friend, Thomas, who went searching for him when he felt the police weren't doing their job. Dawson rolled his eyes. He hated it when civilians took it into their own hands to do the work of a cop. He understood the frustration of not getting answers as quickly as he wanted, or even feeling that no one was putting in the effort, but sometimes answers just didn't come right off, and it took some real digging.

He pulled a map of Connecticut toward him. The victim had been found in Branford, but that didn't guarantee that he was dumped there or even killed there. He studied the Connecticut coastline.

At least he knew that the first victim was last seen in Madison. Not so far from Branford that it wouldn't be unheard of for the body to travel that distance. He needed tide charts for the last year to see if he could get a greater grasp on which direction the body would have come from. He certainly could Google tidal charts, but he wouldn't have a clue as to what he was looking at. He needed to find someone who could read currents, but that meant he'd have one more obstacle that prevented him from getting some immediate answers.

He leaned back in his chair and closed his eyes.

This was going to be a long case if he couldn't start finding some answers. He hoped Ali was having better luck. He opened his eyes when his phone vibrated with a text from her.

You okay?

He tapped in his answer. *Yup. Tired, frustrated and cranky.*

Her reply came back quickly. *Time for a few hours off. Let's take them. I've got lunch. Meet me at my office.*

Dawson sent a thumbs up and stood. It was too early for lunch, but Ali must have something up her sleeve. He was getting nowhere fast, and he needed to talk through some of the issues with the case, and Ali was always the best listener and forced him to think outside the box. He couldn't imagine how he had survived work without her in his life. He smiled.

Just like he thought, Ali had something up her sleeve. She wouldn't answer his questions and used driving as an excuse. Ali didn't say much as she was driving, and Dawson watched the scenery go by, also being silent. The radio was turned up, allowing the two of them to relax. After about twenty minutes, Ali turned it down.

"Do you want to talk about last night?" Her voice was soft, and he could hear the pain in it. Ali was so tuned in to his feelings, more so than *he* was most of the time.

"I'm angry." He clipped his answer.

"Tell me something I don't know." Ali smiled. "Are you angry at Sara or at yourself?"

"Sara." He drew in a deep breath. "I don't get why she's doing this. I miss her and want her back in my life, and she's playing games with me."

"She must have a reason."

Dawson stared at her. "You think she has a good reason for these ridiculous notes she leaves me without showing herself? I know she's out there watching me when I get the notes. I can feel her presence, but she won't answer." He clenched his hands into fists, then slowly unfolded his fingers, exhaling. "What possible reason could she have?"

Ali sighed. "I know you're angry, Wes, but you can't let this eat at you. Obviously, she needs this to be on her timeframe. You're going to have to let it go. Stop looking for her and just wait for her to make her move."

"Not like I have a choice." He reached out and placed his hand on her thigh. "I'm sorry. I don't mean to take it out on you."

Ali grabbed his hand and squeezed it. "I know you don't. And because I'm such a great girlfriend, I'm taking you to Cornfield Point for a picnic lunch and at least a few hours of relaxation."

Dawson grinned. "I haven't been there since I was a kid. I used to love going there." He reached for the radio dial and turned up the music again. He needed this, and he vowed to himself that this lunch would not have any conversation of murder investigations.

He opened the trunk and grabbed the blanket that Ali had brought and walked hand in hand with her down to the beach. It was a gorgeous winter day, and although the sun was shining as per the weather in New England, a cool ocean breeze made him glad that he'd brought his ski jacket.

They settled down on the blanket and just

watched the waves lap at the sand. The ocean was Dawson's happy place, and he was finding that Ali enjoyed it as much as he did. It had become their practice to walk along a beach as often as they could.

As they both sat there, holding hands, Dawson was thankful they didn't need to talk. He felt the tension leave his shoulders, and he began to relax. "Thank you for this," he whispered.

"We both needed it." Ali turned to face him. "Let's walk. I just wish it was warmer so I could kick off my shoes and walk in the water."

"Even if it was warmer, you know that water would be freezing."

She laughed. "But you don't feel it as soon as your feet go numb."

Dawson shook his head. "I'll never understand your desire to have your feet in ice-cold water any time of the year."

"I can't believe you're a native and can't stand the cold water." She pulled him up and started heading down the beach. He held her hand, and they walked at the edge of the water.

thirteen

The day before had been a long day. It started out terrible but got better with a few hours away with Ali. Dawson had gotten home late, but Ali got there even later, closer to midnight. She'd told him that taking a few hours off had put her behind a bit as her workload never seemed to lessen. They'd both fallen into bed and had gone straight to sleep.

Dawson awoke to the smell of coffee being brewed. He reached for Ali, but already knew that she was no longer in bed and might have already left. Sometimes the woman kept worse hours than he did. He showered quickly and headed for the kitchen. There she was, leaning against the counter, holding out a coffee cup to him. Not a travel one, but an actual coffee mug.

"I figured you'd be running into the office." Dawson grabbed the mug and gave her a lingering kiss. "Thank you."

"I thought we ought to take a few minutes to finish that conversation we started yesterday, and honestly, with how late we got home last night, I don't mind going in a little later." She poured herself coffee, and they moved to the living room to sit.

"Okay, let's hear it. I need to see a shrink after these cases." Dawson shook his head. This was not what he wanted to deal with.

"Maybe not a shrink, but I was thinking maybe you, or we, should talk to a person who does past life regression." Ali eyed him, obviously waiting for his reaction.

"Are you kidding me? Ali, you can't possibly believe that we're dealing with reincarnated killers."

She shrugged. "You don't believe a person can live multiple lives?"

"Nope. Do you?"

"Yeah, I do. I think it's possible, and there's a lot of evidence out there to substantiate it." Ali paused. "You can't deny that Beth clearly at the end thought she was Lizzie, and even you said after you interviewed her that she suffered from bad headaches. She also mentioned having memories that she didn't remember."

"I don't know, Ali. It seems too out there." Dawson drank his coffee. "Who do you even talk to about that? Maybe these killers are just crazy—did some research on killing and found these killers that they wanted to emulate."

"Don't rule it out. What else do you have to go on

right now?" Ali asked.

"Well, that's the problem. I've got nothing. I'll give it some thought, but if I need to talk to some past-life regression person, you'll be there with me. You obviously know more about this mumbo-jumbo stuff than I do."

"Open your mind, Wes, you never know what you might learn."

He just shook his head as he rose and held out his hand to her. "Time for work. I obviously have a lot of things to investigate."

They both headed for their respective cars to part ways for the day. As Dawson drove to the Branford Station, he pondered the possibility of reincarnation. He never believed in it, yet there were things that seemed to be explained by the prospect of reincarnation. Maybe Ali was right in having such an open mind about such possibilities, though that lead to *everything was possible*, and when solving crimes, Dawson needed evidence, not an open mind. He'd leave the reincarnation research to Ali if she really wanted to go that way, but for now, he was searching for hard evidence that would give him the answers he needed to actually arrest the killer.

With only one body at the moment, Dawson couldn't even say this was a serial killer, yet there was a niggling in the bottom of his gut that told him to be prepared for more bodies to come. His own boss was ready to pull him from this case, since he felt Dawson could be better served elsewhere, but thankfully, in more ways than one, there were no other homicides that needed investigating at this time in the

State of Connecticut. Therefore, Dawson was given some leeway to continue this case.

He arrived at the Branford Station and started for the conference room. When he got there, Captain Harris had left message for Dawson to find him as soon as he came in. When he went into Harris's office, he found a couple waiting for him.

"Detective Dawson." Captain Harris rose and gestured to him. "This is Mr. and Mrs. Stone. They just arrived home from a trip overseas and was told by their neighbor that you had been looking for them."

"Sir, ma'am." Dawson spoke softly. "Have a seat."

Captain Harris moved around his desk and headed for the door. "I'll let you use my office." Without waiting for a response, he shut the door behind him.

"Detective, what is this about?" Mr. Stone asked. "Cheryl called us on our vacation and told us you were looking for us. We came right home, assuming you had news on Charlie."

Dawson leaned against the captain's desk, facing the couple. "Yes, sir. Unfortunately, I hate that you had to cut short your time away, but we did find your son."

"Where is he?" Mrs. Stone asked fearfully.

"I'm so sorry, Mrs. Stone, but Charlie was found dead. He's still at the medical examiner's office awaiting your arrival to give a positive identification."

Mrs. Stone closed her eyes and tears rolled down her cheeks. "I knew it. I just knew he was dead, but I couldn't stop hoping." Mr. Stone grasped her hand, trying to comfort his wife, but obviously struggling himself to stay composed.

"Take your time, and when you're ready, I can

take you to the medical examiner's office." Dawson placed his hand on Mr. Stone's shoulder before leaving the room.

Captain Harris was waiting in the hallway. Dawson nodded, indicating they had been told. "This wasn't the way I was hoping to meet with them. Not sure I should be thankful or annoyed for interfering neighbors."

"I get that. Though I know if it was my son, I'd be thankful that someone called me home. They've waited long enough for news that they shouldn't have to wait even another day."

Once the Stones had composed themselves, they exited the captain's office. They followed Dawson in their own car to Leighton where the medical examiner's office was located. Dawson had given Ali a call while they were on the way to forewarn her that Charlie's parents were coming to ID the body.

Once the Stones made the confirmation that it was their son, they gave Ali all the information of the funeral home that would be contacting her to retrieve the body. Apparently, they'd been prepared for this. They had already started funeral arrangements and seemed to be looking forward to closure after six long months of the unknown.

fourteen

Ali thought back to her conversation with Wes and reincarnation. She knew he thought she was nuts when it came to this stuff, but she truly believed that reincarnation was feasible. If serial killers could possibly come back in another life, then they probably would still have the ingrained behavior to kill again.

As soon as she arrived at the office, she sat down at her computer and started researching reincarnation. She was fascinated by what she was finding and knew the next step would be to meet with someone who specialized in it. She also knew that Wes would no doubt prefer that she do this research as opposed to him. Normally, she wouldn't be that inclined to do research for a detective, but on the other hand, she wasn't involved with any other detectives, and she loved working with Wes on his cases.

From what she was learning, there were a few different theories on reincarnation. Some people believed that good people reincarnated into better lives, and some believed that it was the opportunity to do better than you had done in a previous life that you had made mistakes in. She liked to think that in her next life she would live a better life and would learn from any mistakes she made in the past. Her biggest fear was that she would be reliving the same mistakes in every life she lived.

She did a quick search for past life regression opportunities locally and found a couple of names within a twenty-minute ride of Leighton. She was tempted to make an appointment but figured she ought to wait and talk with Wes first. She needed to make sure he was truly on board with finding out more. She had a gut feeling this could be a key to the Lizzie Borden case and this one that was resembling features of Lavinia Fisher and the legend of her exploits as the first American female serial killer.

She pushed her research aside and turned to making arrangements for Charlie Stone's body to be picked up. She then went into the autopsy room to start in on the case load she had for today. Simple straightforward autopsies from deaths at the hospital during the night. It would be a fairly easy day in light of what she dealt with on murder investigations and the unknowns that came with reviewing those bodies. At least these corpses had names already known.

fifteen

I had purchased a new padlock, although I was a bit worried that it was too new and would catch my brother's eye on the barn door. I hoped that it would be far enough away from the house that he wouldn't notice it. I knew he was still out of town, so when I arrived at the house, I drove around outback and parked next to the barn.

I got out of my car and looked behind the barn for a back entrance. I found another side door that was locked with another rusty lock, which I'd have to get a replacement for if I was to use this door instead of the front one.

With the need to explore more of the area, I headed for the woods behind the barn and walked just a short distance behind the first thicket of trees.

I came to a small road. It wasn't maintained, and grass had grown tall through it, but ruts were still visible from past use.

I walked down the road to see where it came out and was surprised to find it emerged onto a side road, not far from where the main road passed by the house. I retraced my steps back to the barn, immediately got in my car, and drove back out the driveway. I turned down the side road, found the overgrown path, and drove down it. With no problems at all, I arrived back at the rear of the barn. I smiled.

Once again, I examined the lock on the back door. It was not a key padlock like the front one had been, but a combination lock that I determined to be the sort you could reset and not have to use factory settings. I thought about things that might be a good combination for the lock, and I tried various combinations, including birthdays of my brother, myself, my parents, and even their anniversary date. Nothing worked. Remembering how forgetful my father could be, I tried all zeros. The lock opened. *Unbelievable.*

I walked out front and replaced the padlock before returning to the back of the barn. I grabbed the large camping lamp I had brought with me and started for the tack room and the trap door. Exhilaration pumped through me as I opened it up, descended the stairs, and flipped on the lamp. The light was bright enough to illuminate the whole room. The room itself was unremarkable and had nothing in it. Bare walls and floor.

I went to the other door that I had left opened, and the smell had dissipated. Light from the lamp helped me get a closer look in the smaller room. The hooks were hanging from the ceiling, and the walls themselves were a stainless steel. I searched around the door and found a thermostat regulator to the right of it that I had not seen before. It was in the off position and it had a freezer or refrigerator setting; I turned it to the freezer setting. Immediately, I heard it click on and cold air started flowing throughout. I had found myself a walk-in freezer.

I returned to my car to retrieve the cleaning supplies I had brought with me. I had bleach, a pail—that I filled with water from the house spigot—a sponge, and a large mop. Returning to the freezer, I washed down the walls with bleach and mopped the floor. Once finished, I rinsed it all the best I could and went out, closing the door behind me. I'd give it a couple of days and return to check the temperature and make sure it was working.

I'd found the storage I had been searching for. It would alleviate any need to make sure Minnie and Ramsay stayed out of the basement and the closet that was down there. My precious closet that currently held a small dorm fridge containing my parts that needed to be kept cold, as well as the drawing I used to chart my collection.

My next dilemma was figuring out how to get the bodies out of the inn without being noticed. I wasn't large in stature by any means, though I wasn't petite either. Dead men certainly were heavy and would be for anyone. I'd already struggled with the few bodies I had been dealing with and needed a way to make things a bit easier.

I closed the trap door and looked around the tack room. It truly was empty. I moved into the main section of the barn and searched each stall. All were empty with no signs of ever being used. I turned and went to each corner of the barn that wasn't part of the stalls or tack room. There was some old equipment, a riding lawn mower—that had been my dad's—stood in one corner, along with a weedwhacker.

I paused at the stairs. The hayloft had concerned me a bit with all the shackles and chains attached to the ceiling rafters and walls, but I slowly started up the stairs one more time. As I got to the top, a flash of memory caught me off guard, and I sank down to the floor, sitting near the top stair. In the memory, I was eight years old. I'd come out to the barn to see my dad and he hadn't seen me. I thought I could sneak up on him and scare him, but instead, I had snuck up the stairs and stopped. Before getting to the top, I had heard him talking. I remembered listening to his words, telling whoever was with him how he couldn't wait to see the life drain out of them.

It had scared me, and I had turned and left the barn, hiding in my room for the rest of the day. That night, my dad came to find me. I never told him I had gone to the barn, but I heard my parents talking later that evening about locking it up. The next day, my brother and I were told that the barn was unsafe to go in anymore. What had he been doing? Did my mother know he had someone chained up in there? Why was there a freezer below the barn?

The excitement I felt from killing suddenly made sense to me. My father had been a killer also, and my mother must have known. I suddenly felt more a part of my family than I had in years. My brother was an unknown. Did he know about our parents? Did he really travel for work, or was he out there killing also?

I stood up from the top of the stairs and walked over to the chains and shackles. I lifted them, ran my hands over them. I moved slowly down the wall. There was a total of three sets of shackles and chains, all hooked to the rafters with rings. I looked to the other side of the loft. There was a small metal cabinet. I hadn't noticed it the other day, but honestly, I'd been a little freaked out by the sight of the chains.

I pried open the door of the cabinet as it had rusted shut a bit. Inside, I found a box of old notebooks. I grabbed them, figuring I could read them later. On the shelf above the box, various tools were spread out. There were a few simple things such as clamps and crops, but there were also some things that I had no idea what they were. They didn't look like something I wanted to find out either. I closed the doors, taking the box with me, and made my way back to my car.

I glanced back at the barn before getting in my car. I finally felt like I belonged to my family, whereas for years, I was sure I was in the wrong family. Until now, I had never fit in.

sixteen

Dawson sorted through the files on the table in front of him. Missing person files, reports on Phelps Enterprises trying to figure out who the owners were, and a business card for the owners of the *Lifeline Inn*. He ran his fingers through his hair and sighed. Somehow, he needed to organize this mess. He pulled his yellow legal pad to him and started a list, prioritizing what he needed to do first. With so many stalled leads, it was hard to prioritize this investigation. Usually leads would dictate his next move.

He set the paper aside and picked up the business card and his phone. Punching in the international number, he prayed whoever was on the other end would not be asleep. He was unsure of where overseas they were. The phone rang several times before it went to voice mail. The recorded message indicated he had reached Ronald Connors, which was the name on the card. He left a brief message to please call him and hung up. Nothing to do with that now, but to wait.

He pulled back to him the missing person file he had started. Charlie Stone had been moved to a different file marked CLOSED FILES. Unfortunately, it was not a happy ending to the case, but at least it was closed. He moved on to the next one: Thomas Levesque. Still no word on that one. He had gotten his cell phone number from his friend, David, but when calling it, a disconnect message came up. He'd been able to find the cell phone carrier and upon calling them found out the number had been disconnected for nonpayment. Another dead end. Although Dawson felt that was a sign that something had happened to him. If still alive, he probably would have paid the bill so he could keep using the phone.

The next missing person on his list was Darren Weldon. He was another New Haven resident, although he'd only lived in New Haven for a little over a year before he went missing. He was originally from California. No calls were made, instead his file said, *no known relatives.*

Dawson started doing a search and found some listings for a few Weldons in the Sacramento area. He dialed the first one. No answer. He went on to the second. He got a voice mail that sounded too young to be a parent, but possibly a sibling. He left a note next to that number on his pad of paper and moved on to the third number.

He was startled when he heard a "hello" on the other end.

"Good afternoon. My name is Detective Wes Dawson of the Connecticut State Police. I'm searching for a Darren Weldon from the Sacramento area. Would you be a relative to him?"

"What's he done?" The female voice became colder than the initial hello.

"Nothing, ma'am. I'm looking to get in touch with him or a family member." Dawson waited.

The silence lingered for a long moment before the woman spoke again. "This is his mother. You said you're from Connecticut? Darren moved there almost two years ago. Is he in trouble?"

"Ma'am, he's not in trouble. We're looking for him because a missing person's report was filed on him from his place of business. Have you heard from him in the last few months?"

There was an audible gasp at the other end of the phone. "I talked to him a couple of months ago. He was loving his job and his new apartment. It's not uncommon for him to go a few months without contact, though. He's busy, and I never want to bother him, so I always wait for him to call me." She was rambling, trying to fill the void, which Dawson viewed as a sign that she was trying to process the news and feared finding out what was going on. He'd seen it way too many times when he contacted families of loved ones regarding bad news.

"Do you have his cell phone number that I can try to track down?" Dawson asked gently. She gave him the number and once again was silent. "Ma'am, is there anyone you can be with right now? We don't know that anything has happened, but we want to follow up on it."

"I'm okay. Darren is my only son. I was a single mom. Can you please keep me posted?"

"Absolutely. I'm sorry, ma'am, but I didn't catch your name."

"It's Pamela, Pamela Weldon."

Dawson wrote the information down. "I'll keep in touch and let you know what we find. I'm going to text you my phone number, so you'll have it and feel free to contact me at any time if you have questions."

"Thank you, Detective." The phone went dead as she had hung up.

Dawson hated this aspect of police work. He never enjoyed being the bearer of bad news, and sometimes news of the unknown was even worse than bad news. There was no closure, only more questions that people tried to stay hopeful for, and the downside of his job was that more times than not, he ended up giving bad news, taking away people's hope for a happy ending.

He then tried the cell phone for Darren. It immediately went to voice mail, which was a good sign that it hadn't been shut off. Dawson stood and headed for the door. It was time to give Darren's apartment and his place of business a visit to get more information. By the apartment's address, Dawson knew it was in a good section of New Haven. At this point, Darren had been missing a month, so hopefully, the landlord hadn't tossed his things out and rented it to someone else.

It wasn't a bad drive to New Haven, and Dawson had some time to think about his next steps. He was trying really hard not to interfere with local police procedures, but he was not impressed with the investigations done on missing persons from this particular city. All three seemed to go cold within a week or two of being reported with very little investigation being done. Dawson couldn't help but wonder if more time and effort had been put into the investigation, would there have been a different ending for Charlie Stone instead of the watery grave he ended up in?

He arrived at the apartment listing for Darren Weldon. It was part of a development of condos that were rented out. Dawson entered the office to find a young woman behind the desk. "Are you the manager, or is the manager available?"

The young girl looked him up and down. "I can show you a rental if you are looking."

Dawson smiled and pulled his badge out of his pocket. "I'm actually looking to get into Darren Weldon's place. Who can open that for me?"

The girl glanced at the badge and rose. She quickly went into an office off to the side, and he heard her speak softly but couldn't make out her words. A middle-aged gentleman accompanied her back to the main area.

"Sir, can I help you? I'm Tim McCade, manager here."

Dawson showed him his badge. "Detective Dawson with the State Police. I'm investigating a missing person by the name of Darren Weldon and was told he rented a place here. I'd like to see it, if possible."

"We had some one here about a month ago from the local police asking questions. They didn't look at it."

"Is it still as it was when he was reported missing?" Dawson asked.

"Yes, sir. Mr. Weldon paid a year in advance. I'll hold it the way it is until his paid-rent time is up. I guess there's no harm in showing it to you if something has happened to him." The man pulled open a drawer and withdrew a master set of keys. "I certainly haven't seen him around for a month or so."

"I appreciate your cooperation." Dawson followed the man over to the condo, which he opened and followed Dawson into. "If you could wait here at the door, until I can look around, please."

The man nodded and stayed put, although he was trying really hard to see into the next rooms. Dawson moved through the living room and kitchen on the main floor. The condo was immaculate with nothing out of place. Furnishings were minimal, but not unexpected for someone that hadn't lived in the state long. Dawson then proceeded upstairs. There were two bedrooms. One had a desk it in, much like a home office, although the desk was the sole piece of furniture. The other room held a bed and a bureau. Dawson opened the closet and found neatly hung suits and some shirts. There was a suitcase up on the shelf.

He pulled open the drawers of the bureau, finding neatly folded clothes, but nothing out of the ordinary. In the bathroom were typical toiletries and towels folded and hung over the rack. There wasn't a thing out of place, which to Dawson indicated either the man was a neat freak or he'd straightened up because he had planned to be away for a bit and had gone on vacation or a weekend away.

Dawson went back downstairs and found Mr. McCade still at the doorway. "Thank you. I haven't found anything that indicates something has happened." Dawson stepped outside and waited for the man to lock the door again. He handed the manager his business card. "Please call me if you hear anything that might be helpful."

"I'm sure I told the other officers everything, but I'll let you know if something comes up."

Dawson sat in his car and looked around. This wasn't a neighborhood where there was a high crime rate. An upper level of middle class lived there. Good neighbors, quiet area, and mostly career-driven people. Most of the condos were rented to single people or couples without children.

Dawson turned toward the advertising company that Darren had worked for. Hopefully, more information would be forthcoming. They were the ones who'd filed the missing person's report when Darren hadn't showed up for work for a couple of days. Apparently, something that was very unlike the man. Less than a ten-minute drive from the condos, and Dawson pulled into Parson's Advertising. It was a small building, with about a dozen cars in the parking lot. He took in everything around the area. The commercial zone was definitely a good neighborhood with high-end, customer-service-based businesses surrounding it.

Dawson stepped inside the front door into a well-furnished and calming entrance way. It had a fish tank to the left side of the room with multiple chairs near it for waiting customers. To the right as he walked in was a receptionist desk, which was empty at the moment. He stepped over to the desk and waited. Within a few minutes, a young man came out.

"Welcome. Do you have an appointment?"

Dawson smiled and showed his badge. "I'm hoping I can talk with the person who filed the missing person report on Darren Weldon."

"We never heard back from the other department. Come back here. Tonia will be the one you want to talk to. She's the owner and filed the report." The young man talked as he walked down the hall to the office at the end. "Tonia, a detective is here to see you about Darren."

Tonia rose and gestured for Dawson to come in. "Thank you, Dan." It was an obvious dismissal to the young man, and as Dawson glanced back, he could see the young man would prefer to stay and listen to every word. Tonia waited until he was gone before she turned her attention to Dawson.

"I'm surprised to hear from someone. I made the initial report, was asked a few questions, and we never heard any more."

Dawson shuddered internally. "I'm sorry about that. I'm with the State Police and have been trying to help the local department here with some of their missing person files." He tried to make it sound like they were just overworked and needed the help as opposed to having dropped the ball.

"I'm happy to help in any way. Darren was one of my best employees and I've missed him desperately this past month."

"Was he an employee that was always on time and didn't miss a day of work?"

"Always. He was one of the first ones in and last one out at night. He worked hard. He had more than proved himself in the time he was here. Not only was he hardworking, he was also intuitive, and a well-valued asset for this company. He had a bright future here and would have quickly rose through the ranks. I was grooming him for a VP position."

"Anyone who would have been unhappy with that?" Dawson asked.

"No. I don't think there was one person in the office that didn't like Darren. The man was the type who got along with everyone and made them all feel that they were the most important person in the business. He would have been one hell of a boss."

"Would have been? You feel he won't be back?" Dawson was curious about her word choice, although he had the gut instinct that she was right.

"It's been a month, and with his work ethic, my gut tells me something has happened." Tonia glanced down at her hands folded on the desk. "I hate thinking that way, but Darren wasn't the guy to take off a few days, and then just show back up like nothing happened. He'd call if he was going to be five minutes late, even if that meant he was still early."

Dawson nodded. "There hasn't been much to go on. Did Darren mention anything to you about going away for a couple of days?" He looked down at his notes. "You reported him missing on a Wednesday, saying he hadn't shown up Monday or Tuesday for work."

"Right. I don't recall him saying that he was doing anything over that weekend. Darren was a hard worker, but he was also very private. He didn't talk about his personal life much, so it's not unthinkable that he wouldn't have mentioned weekend plans... at least to me. As you can see, Dan likes to talk, he may know something else that I don't regarding weekend plans for Darren."

Dawson stood. "Thank you for your time. If you don't mind, I'd like to ask Dan a few questions as I'm leaving."

"Oh, go ahead. I'm sure he's dying to find out exactly what's going on. He keeps track of the office personnel as much as possible."

Dawson shook her hand and left his business card with her. He found Dan at the front desk, trying to look busy, although it was obvious he was waiting for Dawson to come back out.

"Any news on Darren?"

Dawson shook his head. "Did you know if he had any plans for that weekend before he was reported missing?"

Dan thought for a moment. "Darren was pretty quiet around here and didn't talk a lot about his personal life. He never told what he was doing on weekends or even talked about what he had done when Monday rolled around. I tried to get him to do things with the few of us that hang out some on weekends, but he always refused. He was never mean about it, just kept to himself."

Dawson nodded. "I appreciate your help. If you think of anything else, Tonia has my number."

Another dead end, it would seem. Frustration filled Dawson as he returned to his car and headed back toward Leighton. He needed to talk with Ali. She had a way of keeping him focused when frustration threatened to overflow.

seventeen

Reading my father's journals had been exciting, and it had taken the edge off the need to kill for me. At least for a little bit. The deeper I got into them, I realized the satisfaction he felt from torturing women. He would pick them up at bars and bring them home. Once they got there, he'd take them to the barn and chain them up. Then, my mother would go and check them out. She made the decision of how they would be tortured and killed.

I was stunned by the lengths my father and mother went to get the women to scream. My father wrote of the loudness and the length of the screaming. He wrote of one woman—from the timeline it must have been the one I heard him talking to—who refused to scream no matter what he did. She would curse at my father, and finally, he killed her by slicing her wrists and letting the blood drain from her until she was dead. It had not been a quick death, but according to the notes, the woman never once begged for her life as the others had done.

I found out that the freezer under the barn had been where the bodies had been kept until they were able to bury them, scattered throughout the five acres of property my parents owned. There had been no mention of my brother or myself in the journals, leading me to believe that my brother never knew. I wondered how he'd feel if he realized he lived in a house that was surrounded by buried bodies. It brought a smile to my face.

I busied myself with preparing for a handful of guests that would be arriving for some winter hiking. I looked through the reservations and smiled as my eyes landed on the name of Kevin O'Neil. The man who had not drunk his whiskey, and thankfully, I had not gone into his room that night to kill. It would be interesting to see if he was any more trusting than he had been the last time. I'd make sure he was in the same room, number one, and hopefully tonight would be a better night for me…maybe not so much for Kevin.

I was busy the next few hours checking in guests and giving them directions for hiking trails for the next morning. Ramsay had made a special cranberry and rum warmer and cute little hors d'oeuvres to reflect the coldness outside. People had started to mingle with the cocktail hour. There was a group of four that were there for hiking tomorrow and another couple that was just passing through on travels

Spikes

and needed to get some sleep before resuming their drive early the next morning. The only one who had not arrived as of yet was Kevin.

I mingled with the guests. This was an act I enjoyed. Pretending to care what people were there for, what they would be doing, but most of all finding out information about their backgrounds. Were they worth taking the risk of killing them? I had never killed a couple before, but it excited me to think about it. I was always so careful not to give any information about myself, and if anyone asked, I expertly steered the conversation back to them, avoiding any personal questions.

I looked up when a gust of cold air came through the room as the front door opened. Kevin stepped in and quickly closed the door behind him. I made my way to the registration desk and met him there. "Welcome back." I smiled warmly at him.

"Good to be back." His smile this time seemed sincere, and he was not as tense as he had been the last stay. Obviously, whatever he had been doing had relaxed him, and he looked like he was more open to conversation.

I handed him his key. "Same room as last time," I said and pointed to the door. "Feel free to drop off your stuff and come have a drink and something to eat."

He nodded and went to the room. I went back to the bar and saw that Ramsay had engaged the group of four into a lively conversation about skiing and they were comparing best slopes that were nearby. I had no idea that Ramsay had even skied. I knew he would leave on his days off, but never asked where he went. Apparently, listening to the conversation, he was more of a snowboarder than a skier, but in my mind, they were really about the same. I was caught up in watching the group talk that I didn't notice Kevin come out from his room until he was standing next to me.

"Can I get you a drink?" I asked.

"Just a beer, please."

I moved behind the makeshift bar and grabbed a bottle of beer for him. Handing it to him, I watched him for a second. "You seem much more relaxed than the last time you were here."

"Seems like a bit of time off from a stress job can do wonders for a person's demeanor." He gave a silent cheer with his beer bottle before taking a drink.

I nodded and glanced around the room. He had not seemed to acknowledge anyone else in the room and didn't seem eager to join in any conversations. That would be a good thing. Made him less rememberable by others. The pain in my head started again.

Tonight. I only heard the one word, but the pain was almost unbearable. The pain whenever those voices came had become worse and worse with every occurrence. I still had no idea whose voice it was. It didn't sound like my father's, yet in some ways, I wanted to believe it was him.

"You're quiet tonight." Kevin's comment broke through my thoughts.

"I'm a people-watcher really. I love these cocktail hours just listening to the guests. That group over there are skiers and apparently get quite animated when telling their stories from past ski trips." I tipped my head toward the other couple that was setting down their glasses and likely getting ready to head to their rooms. "They're just travelers here for a quick sleep before leaving early to hit the road again." I paused and looked at him. "And then, there's you, who I haven't been able to figure out yet."

Kevin laughed. "I prefer not to be studied. I'm just here because I enjoyed this place when I was passing through before and thought I'd stay one more night before I went back to the grindstone Monday."

"I'm glad you came back." I gave a shy smile. I wasn't the greatest flirt, but I hoped he would think I was coming on to him.

For the next hour, Kevin and I listened to the skiers talk and watched Ramsay start to close the bar. As the group went back to their rooms, I collected glasses and trash to take to the kitchen. Kevin finished up his beer and helped pick up the trash. As I started to the kitchen, I turned to him. "Do you want another beer before we close up the kitchen?"

"Sure."

"I'll grab it. Be right back." Ramsay was gone from the kitchen when I got back there. I opened the beer and put my special ingredient in it. Tonight was going to be the night. I couldn't let this fine specimen get away this time. I returned to the sitting room where Kevin was waiting.

"Is there anything else I can do to help out?"

I smiled. "No. Everything's done. I just need to do a bit of paperwork before I head to bed myself."

He seemed to hesitate like he wanted to say more, but then turned toward his room. He glanced back over his shoulder. "Thanks for the beer. I guess I'll see you in the morning."

"Sweet dreams." I smiled as he went into his room. Oh, sweet dreams they would be, and I would make sure of it after he finished his beer. I figured I'd give him a couple of hours, and then pay him a visit.

I worked on the paperwork for the guest checking out in the morning, printing off receipts. After I finished, I glanced at my watch. It had been about an hour and half. I sat still and listened. There was no sound coming from his room. I rose quietly and stood outside his door; my ear pressed against it. No sound at all except for some soft snoring, which was a good sign. He was asleep, and with any luck, he had finished his beer.

I opened the door softly and peeked in. The room had a soft light from the moon shining in. I could make out his silhouette. He was lying on his back with one arm over his head. I quietly closed the door behind me and approached his bed. I didn't bother with a hook for this one. He hadn't said the blasted words, yet I was drawn to him. He was fit and had the body of a man who cared about his health. Not only was his torso perfect, but I had never seen a man with such perfectly shaped ears that were close to his head without sticking out too far. Could he be a two-for-one?

I stood over him. I hated to mar his body, but it was inevitable with the spikes. I would make him a great shirt that would cover those imperfections left from his death. He must have sensed my presence as his eyes slowly opened. They held mine for a moment before he became fully aware that I was next to him.

"Yes, I am here." Recognition came into his eyes. Eyes could be so full of emotion. They showed fear, sadness, excitement. Right now, his had started to fill with fear. "Were you thinking of me?"

He tried to move and realized he was paralyzed. I picked up the *empty* beer bottle. "I'm so sorry. I just couldn't let you get away a second time. You didn't bother to drink your whiskey on your last visit, so I had to watch you leave."

He was afraid, yet another emotion was showing. *Anger.* "Don't be angry, Kevin. You are the perfect one." I ran my fingers along his jawline and down his chest. Oh, the muscles. I could see rage overtake the fear in his eyes. I'm sure he was cursing me in his mind.

I leaned down and gave him a kiss on his lips. I couldn't resist. I didn't usually have this much contact with my victims, but he hadn't upset me. This one…I just *wanted* him. I sat next to him on the bed and wondered how I could keep him alive. My mind wandered to the barn and the chains and shackles hanging in the loft. How I would love to be able to see this man daily. Part of me didn't want him to die.

Do it! The voice shouted in my head, and the pain was almost unbearable. I held my head and closed my eyes.

You need to do it now. Stop getting attached to these people. The angry voice sounded almost violent.

I shook at the forcefulness of the words in my

head, then stood and looked down at Kevin. "I'm sorry." I pressed the button and the bed fell to the side.

Kevin dropped directly onto the spikes, dying instantly. I pressed the button again to pull the bed back up, straightened the room, and took the beer bottle to the kitchen. Then I returned to his room and took all his possessions with me to the cellar where he awaited. It was just a little after one a.m.

I placed his things aside and stood over him. He was gone, yet the beauty of him remained. I lowered the spikes, unimpaling him. I cleaned his body from the blood that flowed and wrapped him in plastic. I put him on a dolly and wheeled him out the back door and to my car. After managing to get him inside it, I went back to the house to be sure no one was awake and slid the bills under the doors of our guests. I shredded Kevin's and deleted his reservation from the computer as well as all traces of his credit card for this particular visit. If searched, his past visit was the only one that would come up.

I knew the couple leaving early would be gone before I was up anyway, so I left for the rest of the evening. I could at least place Kevin in the barn freezer so I could enjoy him a little while longer.

eighteen

It was Saturday and Dawson awoke to Ali snuggled close to him. He watched her as she slept and wondered how he got so lucky to have this woman next to him. They both had agreed that for the first time in a long time they were going to take the day off. While Dawson appreciated Ali's work ethic and the love she had for her job, with both of them having such busy and demanding jobs, it was a challenge sometimes to make the time they needed for each other.

He slid slowly out of bed, careful not to disturb her. He smiled at the memory of last night, when they'd done everything *but* sleep. It had been a while, but his desire for Ali never faltered.

He grabbed a pair of sweatpants and slid them on before quietly closing the bedroom door to let

Ali sleep. He went to the kitchen and started coffee. While it brewed, he perused the refrigerator. Though he hadn't shopped in a while, Ali obviously had brought some provisions because there was fresh bacon, eggs, and a new bottle of orange juice. Leave it to her to think of what they would need today.

He pulled out the bacon and started frying it up for breakfast. When the bacon was finished, he poured himself a cup of coffee and sat down to read the newspaper. He scanned the obituaries out of habit. He'd started doing that before Sara began leaving him notes. Although he knew she was alive, he still went over the obits, just in case. He sighed and moved to the daily news. There was an article about crime on the rise in surrounding areas and another on the lack of police officers present in those areas due to budget cuts and layoffs. Economy hopefully would improve soon, otherwise things were just going to go from bad to worse in those neighborhoods.

He'd just finished reading the sports sections when Ali came out of the bedroom wearing an old sweatshirt of his that came to just above her knees. He whistled at her.

She grinned and blew him a kiss. "You didn't have to let me sleep. It feels so late."

Dawson chuckled. "Nine o'clock is not late… well it is for us normally, but you needed it. We've both been burning the candle at both ends, and your workload just seems to get heavier and heavier. They really need to hire another person in your office."

Ali grabbed a mug and filled it with coffee. "Yes, they do, but you and I both know that isn't going to happen, not with all these budget cuts still going on." She reached for a slice of bacon before she sat down with her coffee, nibbling the bacon.

"Hungry? Want me to cook omelets?" Dawson asked.

"Just coffee right now. Maybe in a bit."

"Just coffee says the woman eating the bacon." Dawson shook his head.

Ali popped the rest of it in her mouth. "I have no idea what you're talking about," she said with a grin.

They drank their coffee as Ali glanced through the newspaper and Dawson pulled out his laptop to check emails. They were silent, but it was a comfortable silence that Dawson had grown to love and missed dearly the days Ali was not there with him. Although, those days were becoming fewer and fewer.

Ali set the newspaper aside. Dawson stood and refilled his coffee mug and turned to fill hers. Ali had sat back and was watching him. "You've got something on your mind."

Ali smiled. "That obvious, huh?"

"Yes. Please don't let it be about the murder or the missing people." He sat back down.

Ali sipped her coffee before responding. "Not technically."

Dawson shook his head. "What happened to no talk of this stuff on our day off?"

"I said not technically. I did some research though on reincarnation and past life regression."

Dawson took a sip of his coffee and waited. This was not a conversation he really cared to have, but

Ali seemed to think it was relevant to the case. "Go ahead."

"Don't sound too enthused." Ali rolled her eyes. "Seriously, Wes. I think this could be useful. Why can't you just be open-minded about it?"

Dawson chuckled. "I'm open-minded…about the fact that you are nuts. Go ahead though, I'm listening."

Ali stuck out her tongue at him. "Nuts is a relative term." She stood up and grabbed the plate of bacon and placed it on the table.

"Do you want something with that?" Dawson asked.

"Naw. Coffee and bacon are good."

"Well, I'm going to cook an omelet while you talk. Save me some bacon."

"Fine. There may be a piece or two left for you." She settled back into her chair, and Dawson started pulling eggs and cheese from the refrigerator.

Dawson cracked a couple of eggs, whipping them while he waited for the pan to heat. He dropped a dime size amount of bacon grease in the pan, and poured in the eggs. He glanced over his shoulder at Ali.

"Okay," she began after a lengthy silence, "so I was looking up reincarnation. There are some different theories to it. Some people talk about good people being reincarnated into better lives, or some believed that it was the opportunity to have a better life than in their previous life that they had made mistakes in."

As Ali talked, Dawson added cheese to the omelet before folding in in half and placing a cover on top of the pan. After a few minutes, he slid the finished omelet on his plate and sat down with it. "Okay, and what does that mean for the case?" He snagged a couple of pieces of bacon before Ali could protest.

"Forget the case for a moment and consider this. What if people could have another life where they could learn from their mistakes? Theoretically, if that was the case, what's to say that a serial killer couldn't come back into another life, and if they didn't learn from their past, they'd continue the cycle of killing."

"Don't you think that's far-fetched?"

"No, I don't. Think about it. Have you ever had moments of déjà vu?"

"Everybody does. What does that prove?"

"That's a sign that you've had a past life." She paused but held up her hand. "I see your mind pushing all that aside and ready to deny it. Please for a moment can you just have an open mind?"

"My mind is open, Ali. I'm not pushing it aside. I just don't think it's something I can believe in. If you believe it, there's nothing wrong with that. But I have a hard time believing that a serial killer is going to come back and continue killing because they aren't smart enough to learn from mistakes." He finished his omelet and reached for the last piece of bacon.

"Maybe they didn't feel that the killings were a mistake. Maybe, like Beth…Lizzie, was killing for a specific reason. That poor girl had been abused by her father and bullied by people around her all her life. She was killing for a very specific purpose. I'm sure she didn't feel that was a mistake. If she was to reincarnate, and bad things continued to happen to her in her new life, would the killing cycle continue?" She paused. "Don't look at me like that. I'm theorizing, not saying that is what I believe happens."

Dawson smiled. "I love the fact that you have these crazy theories and yes, I do think about them after we have these conversations. But I also realize you have your moments of lunacy, but it's one of the many things I love about you."

Ali smiled. "Good. You love my craziness. Therefore, I would like to have an adventure today."

Dawson groaned. "I walked right into this one. What adventure do you want?"

"I want to meet with a someone who practices past life regression and get their opinion of it."

"You already know their opinion. If they practice it, they believe it." Dawson looked at her. "If this is what you want to do, we'll do it."

She grinned at him. "I thought you might say that, so I scheduled us an appointment at one this afternoon."

nineteen

Dawson and Ali approached the office for *Remembrance*. The waiting room had all kinds of interesting paraphernalia. Dawson walked around while Ali let the receptionist know they were there. Crystals, rocks, salt lamps, and so much more had Dawson shaking his head. How could Ali truly buy into this thought process that people lived a past life?

Dawson turned toward Ali about the time a young woman came down the hallway. She held out her hand to Ali, "Selene Rossman."

"Ali Jenson, and this is Wes Dawson." He smiled. He noticed that Ali had not mentioned he was detective. "We had some questions regarding the past life regression and we hoped you could answer them for us."

"Are you looking to book a session, either of you, or both of you?" Selene glided right past the *answer question's* part.

"I've always wanted to, but we have questions as I don't know that much about it. Could you answer them? I did book you for the time of a session, but at this point, I just want to get my questions answered."

Selene smiled and gestured to the hallway. "Right this way."

Dawson smirked. Obviously, the mention that she was still getting paid whether or not she made up some story was okay by her. They followed her down the hallway into a small room. There was a table and a few chairs scattered around the room.

Upon closing the door, Selene turned toward them. "Please make yourselves comfortable, and I will walk you through what we would be doing if you decided to discover your past."

Dawson chose a chair on the other side of the table, and Ali pulled up a chair closest to the desk in the corner. Selene sat down at the desk and focused on Ali. "What makes you think you want to discover your past?"

"Well…" Ali glanced at Dawson before turning back to Selene. "I always get déjà vu and feel like I remember things that just don't seem to fit with my life."

"Those can definitely be signs of someone having lived a past life." Selene looked at Dawson. He had sat back and stretched his legs out in front of him. He was trying hard to give the impression that he was interested, but more of a bystander and didn't really want to be involved in the conversation. "Mr. Dawson, have you had these feelings also?"

He cleared his throat. "I can't say that I have, but I'm not always the most intuitive person." He rested his eyes on Ali and a small smile played on her lips. Oh she was enjoying this, and he would be sure that she made up this little charade to him when they got home.

Ali broke eye contact and returned her attention back to Selene. "Wes just wants to be sure I am not being taken in for my beliefs. He is a bit skeptical."

Selene nodded. "That happens a lot. Not everyone has had the experience of living a past life, and those who haven't tend to be less believing than those who have lived through a life more than once. I have had clients that have had two or three lives."

"Really?" Ali sat up. "Can you tell when you meet someone if they have had a past life? I mean—could I tell if I met someone on the street?"

Dawson silently applauded Ali's enthusiasm. They had talked in the car about what kind of questions should be asked, and Ali certainly didn't come across as being interrogative, but more inquisitive.

"It's not always that easy. Sometimes we will feel drawn to a certain person or place because it is familiar to us in a past life. Someone's behavior wouldn't necessarily tell you if they have had a past life."

Ali nodded. "I understand. What is the process that you do to find out about a past life, if I was to book an appointment?"

Selene gestured toward the table. "You would be lying on the table. I typically place a blanket over you as sometimes you can get cold as you regress to another lifetime. We will count down and you will go under a trance, but at this time you are fully aware of what is going on. Your mind is open, but you can stop at any time. I will ask you questions about what you see, etc. I will not lead you with questions, but from your answers we can determine where you are time-wise and go from there. Usually my clients guide the session by just telling me what they see. At any time if you see something you don't want to see, you simply can ask to leave and we will take you out of that moment in time. Most often, my client still wants to see things that are upsetting, but instead of going through it, they rise above and watch as a bystander."

Ali was nodding and watching Selene intently. Dawson struggled not to roll his eyes. It was all a bunch of mumbo-jumbo to him, but Ali was intrigued. He knew that look. She'd want to come back for this. He would have to be supportive even if he didn't believe in it. He would never want to hold her back from learning things about herself, even if it was just how gullible she could be.

Dawson's mind drifted, thinking of Ali, as Selene went on with her spiel of what Ali could expect. He was brought back to the moment when Ali stood up and shook Selene's hand. He stood up and did the same. "Thank you for your time."

She nodded at him. "Macy can help you at the front desk, Ali."

Dawson didn't say a word until they were back in the car. He had stood outside waiting while Ali made an appointment for her own past life regression. When she came out, he opened the car door for her and waited for her to slide in before shutting it. Once he was in and they had gotten back on the road, he glanced at her. She was sitting there with a smirk on her face, watching him.

"What?"

"Oh, nothing. I'm just waiting for the snarky comments." She giggled and shook her head.

"I'm not going to say any. If you're interested in this and want to do it yourself, I support you." He kept his eyes on the road and a smile on his face, as he could feel her gaze on him. Ali reached over and laid her hand on his thigh. She slowly rubbed up and down, a barely perceptible movement.

By the time they drove back into Wes's driveway, Ali could see he was starting to squirm a bit. She stopped caressing his leg as he put the car in park, and he turned toward her. She smiled and crooked a finger at him to follow her, then she slipped from the car and was almost to the door before he even got out of the car.

He quickly unlocked the door and held it open for her. She kicked off her shoes just inside the door, faced him, and grabbed onto the collar of his shirt, pulling him toward her. She kissed him softly, then backed away before he could deepen the kiss. Still holding his collar, she walked backward, taking him with her until they reached the bedroom.

Inside the bedroom, she temptingly unbuttoned his shirt, sliding it off his shoulders. She reached down and unbuttoned his jeans, unzipping them slowly, before pushing them down so he could step out of them. She firmly nudged him toward the bed where he sat down and waited, watching her with eyes that said, *your turn.*

Ali smiled and teasingly lifted her shirt over her head. She threw it at him, and reached behind her to unhook her bra. Wes groaned and Ali smirked. She coyly stripped the rest of her clothes and walked leisurely to him.

His hands rested on her hips as she took his head in both hands and kissed him. Her tongue teased him and the kiss deepened. She gave a small laugh when he picked her up and rolled her onto the bed so she was under him. Their gaze locked and she beheld a mutual love in Wes's eyes, right before he claimed her lips.

twenty

Dawson arrived at the scene at the Madison Cannery. He had been called and asked to come with no
real explanation of what was going on. He pulled up
and parked across the street, out of the way of the
firetrucks and ambulance that had just arrived. He
jogged across the street and found the Madison Chief
of Police standing by the door of the cannery. He
raised a hand, motioning for Dawson to approach.

"What's going on, sir?" Dawson asked, glancing
around. There was a small sedan that had hit a tele-
phone pole. The car was demolished, and the pole
had fallen, causing live wires to be down so that the
driver couldn't exit the vehicle.

The chief frowned. "My guy on duty was called
to the scene. This cannery has been closed for the

longest time, yet when the fire department arrived they had to call the electric company to turn off the power. The power lines had caused a short in the cannery and a fire ensued. The firemen were working diligently to remove the driver from the car. Once they realized there was still power going to the cannery, they went in. They gave me a call because of some unusual findings and I decided it was time to call you in with what we found."

The chief gestured for Dawson to move ahead of him into the building. "Straight back to that back room over there."

They moved to the door on the opposite side of the room. There was a lot of standing water from the fire being put out. When Dawson got to the door, he glanced at the police chief. He gestured for Dawson to open it. Dawson pulled the door open, and they stepped into a work room. There were workbenches with knives hanging above them. On the opposite wall to the door was a freezer door.

"That's the one." The chief gestured to the door.

Dawson walked over and pulled the door open. There were two bodies lying on the floor. Dawson took a step closer. He pulled out his cell phone and sent Ali a text: *Get to the Madison Cannery, 2 new bodies.*

The bodies looked like they'd been killed by Dawson's unknown killer. Body pieces were missing from both of them, but only one of them had a hook in his cheek. One body was missing his scalp, and the other his facial skin. Dawson turned toward the chief.

"You found these because of the fire?"

"Yes, sir. They would have been left here for quite

a while. This place has been out of business for the last fifteen years, but for some reason the electricity was still running to the freezer."

Dawson glanced back at the bodies. "Who would have had access to this place after it closed? I'll have to check with the electric company on who's paying the bill."

The chief shrugged. "I wouldn't know who still had access here, but the door wasn't locked, so anyone could have come in and out without true access."

Dawson nodded. "Let's get out of here and wait for the ME to show up."

Dawson stood outside the building by the door, waiting for Ali. He watched as they cut apart the car, finally getting the driver out and placing him on a stretcher. He was alive. It was a one-car accident, fortunately, with no one else being involved or in the car with the driver. Small miracles, and a big break for this case that the car knocked out the electricity and started a fire in the building. Otherwise, they may have never found these bodies. This was going to greatly add to Ali's workload and Dawson knew that meant they wouldn't be seeing each other for the next few days.

Ali arrived within the hour after Dawson had sent the text. He led her to the freezer to examine the bodies.

Ali took in the scene and squatted down between the two bodies. "It will be hard to determine time of death or even how long they have been here. Being frozen has preserved them nicely, but that will mess up pinpointing when they actually died."

Dawson nodded.

"Do you think either of these are the missing men you've been looking for?" Ali asked.

"Unsure right now, but I would guess they are." Dawson sighed. "Three bodies now and no leads."

"You'll solve it. You always do." Ali smiled. "And don't say it...I know, but *will you before we find more bodies*...You will."

Dawson grinned at her. "Stop acting like you know me so well."

He moved to the side as Ali's assistant came in with body bags and a gurney to take the bodies to the van and back to the morgue. "I'll keep you posted," Ali said.

twenty-one

I turned on the news, as it was a quiet night with not many guests. The man was just starting a story about a car accident and an electrical fire that ensued from the electric wires coming down. It was at the Madison Cannery. I shook my head. This was not working out. I had one more spot to use, and I was confident that the last spot would not be found anytime soon.

I sat back and closed my eyes. The migraines were worse lately, and I couldn't figure out why. I still had the voice in my head telling me to *finish it*. Whatever that meant. I had continued to read my father's journals about his killings and the way he did things, his disposal of the bodies. Each journal laid out exactly where the bodies had been buried, and although scattered around the five acres of property, each body would be able to be located if anyone wanted to find them.

I had felt a closeness with my father these past few days while reading his encounters, and I was fascinated by the precision he wrote about with each one, and how each killing was different for him. However, I was still confused as to how the man was in my thoughts. It wasn't my father, and the voice got louder with each one of my kills. The voice was addicting at times and impossible to ignore.

All I could piece together so far was that whoever this was, it had brought me to a different type of killing than what my father had done, yet the familiarity that I felt from hearing his voice made me realize he was much more to me than just a man. He had held a special part of my heart, but that was all I knew regarding this man.

I had moved all my special containers of body parts and my chart to the barn and the room under the tack room. It was a much better location, and I no longer had to worry about Ramsay or Minnie finding anything, not that either one of them went to the basement or even knew about the button to release the bed or the spikes below it. I loved having this little secret all to myself. I felt superior to them, knowing about the hidden room downstairs and all that had been happening right under their noses, and they didn't have a clue.

I blinked to bring myself out of my daydream and refocus as to what was being said on the television. Three bodies had been found. By all intents and purposes, the police informed that they were looking at a serial killer and advised people from going places alone, or if they knew anything to call the Branford Police Department with information. I cringed at the thought of all the people who would call in saying they had information, but then just giving false information, hoping to get their fifteen minutes of fame. On the plus side, as long as the police were chasing false leads, I had more time to continue with my plan.

It had been a few weeks since my last kill, and I could feel the itch for it building inside of me. The unexplained need for seeing the fresh blood run down the spikes, to see the panic and fear in the victim's eyes when they realized they were paralyzed and helpless to me. I needed two more men to complete my project. But they had to be perfect.

I looked through the upcoming registrations. Very few single men coming in. With any luck, a few stragglers without reservations would show up. Unfortunately, coldness had arrived, along with a heavy snowfall that had happened over the past few nights. It would be hard for anyone to walk to the inn, and that led to the questions of how to dispose of their vehicles. I hoped the snow would leave soon and that the hiking trail would reopen.

I needed something to happen as quickly as possible. The anxiety of not knowing when my next kill would be had me feeling like I could jump out of my skin.

twenty-two

Ali had the two victims out on the autopsy tables. This first young man was missing his scalp. Care had been taken to make sure the scalp remained intact as far as Ali could tell by the pretty smooth area left. There was no hook in the cheek, which was different from the first victim. The second young man had his facial skin removed, again made with very precise cuts, but keeping the face intact beneath the skin. This one had a hook in his cheek that obviously had been placed after the facial skin was removed.

She took her usual measurements and several photographs of both bodies. They had the same puncture marks as the first fish-hooked corpse. She had no doubt this was the same killer. Suddenly going from one body to three was a bit much, especially when it was pure chance, they had found these bodies.

Ali finished her autopsies and headed back to her office to write the reports. It was going to be a long night. She finished up the reports and started loading the images she had taken into the data base to run against the missing persons pictures that Dawson had created. She hated finding missing people this way. It was never the ending that their family had hoped for, and just meant that there was closure, but in the most unbearable way.

While she waited for the pictures to run through the program, she started pulling up images of spikes. She tried to match the puncture wounds to fence spikes, spears, and anything else she could find that could make a wound like those on the bodies. No matches. She rubbed her eyes in frustration. She stood and started out of her office when she ran into Wes.

"Where are you going?" He wrapped his arms around her and pulled her close.

"Needed some coffee. Running pictures of the victims to your missing persons data base to see if we can get a match for them. I've tried searching for some sort of weapon that would leave the type of puncture marks that have been on all the victims and have come up with nada."

"You haven't eaten yet either, have you?"

Ali shook her head. "Since when do you have time to take out of your investigation to see if I have eaten?"

Wes laughed. "Since I haven't eaten either, and I brought up some Greek food and water for you. No coffee."

"Now that sounds familiar, and now I feel like you're just being spiteful because I took your coffee away."

Wes steered her back into her office. "Not at all. Just looking out for you."

He pulled out two containers from the bag he had been carrying. Grilled chicken over rice with tzatziki sauce, with a side salad and warm pita bread. It wasn't long before they were both eating in silence.

"I need to map out the body parts that have been taken so far," Ali said, breaking the quiet. "Eyes, scalp, face. All parts of the face, but for what end?"

Wes grimaced. "Victor Frankenstein on our hands, creating their perfect monster?"

Ali looked up at him. "I don't know if we're dealing with Victor. I think he learned his lesson. But I've been reading, and these puncture wounds seem to be significant to Lavinia Fisher, the one we talked about earlier."

Wes held up his hand. "I do *not* want to be chasing another ghost. Tell me you're not going to suggest that we have another Lizzie Borden on our hands."

Ali raised her hands in surrender. "Not Lizzie Borden. You already got her."

Wes waited and watched her. Ali smiled at him. "Are you ready to hear my theory?"

"With bated breath, my dear." He rolled his eyes.

"We should talk more about Lavinia Fisher"

"What about her?"

"Well, only if you want a little insight to our killer." Ali grinned before continuing. "Lavinia Fisher, I *think*. She died in 1820. The legend is that she and her husband had an inn of sorts. They would rob people who stayed there, but there were also rumors that she killed them. She was considered the first American female serial killer." She took a sip of coffee. "But here's the interesting part. According to the legend, she would slip them some sort of sleeping herb in their tea, and then she would drop them from their beds—I guess the bed would drop out from under them—onto a bed of spikes."

"What? That's sadistic."

Ali smiled. "Yes, it is, but it would match up with the puncture marks I'm seeing on the victims. As far as what I've been able to read, she didn't take body parts as trophies."

Wes grinned. "Puncture wounds, maybe it's a vampire we're dealing with."

Ali rolled her eyes. "Would you be serious?"

"It's hard to be serious when you are talking about century-old killers. If this is a copycat, would they necessarily do everything the same way, or could taking trophies be part of incorporating their own style to it?"

As they were finishing up, Ali's computer beeped, indicating a match had been found. She opened the screen and it displayed the picture of the victim without the hook in his cheek, alongside the photo of Thomas Levesque. She glanced at Wes and found he'd also been looking at the screen.

He sat back in his chair and frowned. "Well, I guess we know what happened to Charlie's friend."

She gestured to the screen. "And here's another match for the other body. Darren Weldon."

Wes sat forward again. "No..." He rubbed his temples. "This is the kid that moved from California and his boss was grooming him for a VP position. Such a waste of a young life."

"Two more missing cases solved." Ali pointed out.

"Yes, but still no leads as to whom the lunatic is that is doing this."

"Two steps forward, two steps back."

Wes smiled. "Want to dance?"

twenty-three

Dawson had a splitting headache. Too late of a night, not enough sleep and now having to inform loved ones that their friend or son had been found. Dawson started with Pamela Weldon. He hated to do this over the phone, but there was no other way to accomplish it.

Dawson dialed her number and listened to the ring. It rang three times before she answered. "Hello?"

"Ms. Weldon?"

"Yes, Detective. I had your number programmed into my phone. Have you found Darren?" The stress in her voice came through the phone loud and clear.

"Unfortunately, Ms. Weldon, we have found him. I don't have a lot of details yet, but there was some foul play involved."

"He's dead? No…" Her voice was overtaken with the sobs that consumed her.

Dawson waited a minute. "Ma'am, I am so sorry for your loss. Do you have someone you can call to be with you?"

"I'm fine. Thank you." She cleared her throat and Dawson could tell she was making every effort to pull herself together. "When can I come get him?"

"At any time, ma'am. An autopsy has been done."

"I'll make arrangements and let you know when I'll be arriving." She was quiet for a moment and Dawson almost wondered if she had hung up. "Thank you, Detective, for calling me."

"I wish it was with better news, ma'am." The call ended, and Dawson stared into space. How awful for a mother to hear the news of her son's death over the phone. He could only imagine what she was going through: her only child.

Dawson stood and headed to the door. He could at least inform David Nielson, the friend of Charlie Stone and Thomas Levesque, in person. At least David could have closure for his two friends.

Dawson drove the distance to New Haven and found David sitting on his front porch just like he had been the last time they'd spoken. David rose as Dawson exited his vehicle.

"I'm hoping you're here with news," David said as he descended the stairs.

"I'm not sure it's the news you want to hear, but yes, we found Tommy."

"He's gone just like Charlie, isn't he?"

"Yes, I'm afraid he is. Is there any other information you can give me about where they might have been?"

"I've got nothing, sir. I knew this wasn't going to be the ending we wanted, but I guess I was kind of hoping when you were around here asking questions that you might bring some good news."

Dawson nodded. "I'm sorry I couldn't do that for you." He stuck out his hand to shake David's, and as the young man grasped his hand and gave it a firm shake, Dawson felt almost no hope as to how he would solve these murders.

twenty-four

Dawson arrived at the police station in the morning and was surprised to see the captain with a middle-aged woman in the conference room that Dawson had been using. When Dawson walked into the room, the captain turned around and faced him. Dawson was a little taken aback when he saw the young woman looking at the board.

"Can I help you?" Dawson moved in front of the board, facing the woman.

The captain smirked. "This is a good friend of ours, Cheryl Porter. Cheryl comes in from time to time to lend a hand in solving some cases, typically missing-person."

Dawson looked at the woman and back to the captain. "Yes?"

"Cheryl came in this morning because she had a feeling you may need some help."

"I'm sorry, I'm not sure I'm following what kind of help you can give, Ms. Porter." Dawson seethed inside. He didn't need someone butting their nose into his business and mucking up the investigation.

"If I may, Detective Dawson, just have a moment of your time." Cheryl spoke softly as she turned to sit in a chair at the table.

Dawson looked at the captain, hoping to get something that would allow him to throw this woman out of his conference room. The captain just smiled and gestured to the table. They both sat down with Cheryl, and Dawson clamped his jaw tight and waited to see what she had to offer.

"Detective Dawson, I know you're dealing with multiple murders that are all related."

"Yes, you saw the press conference," Dawson replied.

"Actually, I didn't. I don't watch much TV. I had a vision." She paused, tipping her head to the side watching Dawson.

Dawson closed his eyes. Great, now he had to deal with a looney who thought she could see the future.

"I saw a young man having a séance," she continued, before he could say anything, "and although he failed to bring back the spirit he most likely wanted to talk to, he opened a portal for other evil spirits to come through. These spirits much like reincarnation, attach themselves to others. I believe your Lizzie Borden case was exactly from this incident."

Dawson shook his head. "I'm sorry, I don't believe

in ghosts or spirits that come to attach themselves to others. This is a murder investigation, and I really don't have time to sit around and talk about spirits." Dawson started to stand.

Captain Harris held up his hand. "Hold on, Dawson. I know this is an unorthodox method of looking at a case, but Cheryl has been very instrumental in solving some of our cold cases. I think you should listen to what she has to say."

Should listen? Dawson sat back down. *Apparently, I don't have a choice* but *to listen.* Dawson's nerves were frayed, and this intrusion into his case grated on his nerves. He didn't say a word, but just waited for this *psychic* to speak.

"You're not a believer. I can see waves of anger and frustration rolling off you."

Dawson sat back silently.

"These cases are all related. They have all been killed in the same fashion by something that causes holes in their body."

"How much information did the captain give you, or did you pick all this up by studying the board?" He pointed to the victimology board. This wasn't news that he didn't already know.

"The captain told me nothing about this case, and yes, I have read the names on your board, but there is nothing up there talking about the way these men died. How would I know about the holes in the bodies?"

Dawson shrugged. "Who knows?"

"This killer is tied to unsolved cases of long ago, not directly, but by family."

Dawson shook his head. "Meaning what?"

"You will need to look into the past to go forward on this case."

Dawson stood. "Thank you for your insight, but at this time I have work to be done." He waited until Cheryl and the captain stood. He moved to the board and turned his back on them, waiting to hear them leave the room. He closed his eyes tight...*what rubbish, look to the past to go forward.* What was the women, some kind of witch?

The door closed quietly, and Dawson turned around. Both the captain and Cheryl were walking across the bull pen toward the captain's office. It had been bad enough for Dawson just chasing ghosts, but now he had all the whackos coming out of the woodwork. What happened to the days where crime was straightforward and could be solved fairly quickly?

twenty-five

Dawson drove straight to the medical examiner's office. He had no sooner reached Ali's office when his phone beeped with a text message. He pulled it out just as Ali came around the corner.

"Well, that was quick."

Dawson smiled. "Was this text from you?"

"It was, just asking you to stop by." She grabbed his hand and continued walking, bringing him with her to the autopsy room.

"I take it you have news for me, which I really need after the conversation I just had at the station," Dawson stated.

"Oh, I can't wait to hear about that, but first, I want you to look at this." Ali pulled out photographs of the three bodies they had found. "What do you see?"

Dawson carefully examined each photo. "Only two of them have hooks in their cheek." He glanced at each one again. "They all have puncture marks in the torso, which only proves that we are dealing with the same killer most likely."

"Yes. I think we are leaning toward the Lavinia Fisher reincarnate."

Dawson shook his head. "This is bullshit. You've got it in your mind that we're dealing with some killer from centuries ago being reincarnated. And the captain brought in a psychic because she had some vision about multiple bodies."

Ali took a step back. "Being closed-minded isn't going to help with this case."

Dawson sighed. "I'm not closed-minded. I'm a realist."

"You can accept this theory and still be a realist." Ali tucked the photos back into a folder. "What's stopping you from looking at every possibility?"

Dawson shrugged. "It's not something I can just believe if I have never believed in spirits and reincarnation before."

"I'm not saying you need to believe, but you can open your mind to other possibilities. I'm not even saying you're chasing a ghost. Whoever is killing is a flesh-and-blood, live person."

Dawson felt Ali's gaze on him, and he closed his eyes. He thought the Lizzie Borden case was out there, but did the psychic have actual information that he could use?

"Wes…" Ali spoke softly.

He turned to face her. "I'm not mad at you. I'm

just angry that there aren't any real leads. And the damn psychic tells me I have to look to the past to go forward. None of this makes any sense."

"What exactly did the psychic tell you?" Ali grabbed his arm and guided him to her office.

"A bunch of mumbo jumbo about looking to the past to solve cases. I don't know. I really just tuned her out."

"First mistake." Ali grinned.

"Oh, please, don't start counting my mistakes in this case. I feel like I'm nowhere near where I have to be to solve this case." Dawson exhaled slowly. "How do we get answers when we can't even pinpoint time of death? I don't mean within a few hours, but can we even narrow it down to maybe the month they were killed?"

"I know you're frustrated. I don't have any time-table in which these murders were committed." Ali sat back in her chair. "And I also know that isn't what you want to hear right now."

"I want facts...something I can work with."

"Okay. But since we don't have a lot of facts to go on at present, why don't you tell me more about this psychic?" Ali asked.

Dawson succumbed. "She was in the conference room when I got there with the captain, looking at my victimology board. I don't know how much the captain told her. She made comments like there were multiple bodies and the killer was tied to past murders. Not directly, but through family."

Ali nodded. "Okay. So do you need to look at past, unsolved murder cases?"

"Do you realize how many unsolved murder cases there are in this state?" Dawson asked.

"I know. Unimaginable. But what if you broke it down to this specific area? You must have a contact back at State Headquarters that can search for the cold cases in this area."

Dawson grinned. "You just want me to work around the clock."

"Not at all. But you and I both know you're at a spot where you have to do something different with this one."

"I'll make a call to Kathy and see what she can dig up for me." Dawson stood. "At least with Beth, Lizzie, whoever, there wasn't a bunch of bodies to be found with no indication of where they had been killed."

"Keep me posted with what you find out."

Dawson leaned down and gave Ali a light kiss. "Get some work done and stop telling me what to do." He smiled and was gone before she could reply.

twenty-six

I spent the last few days trying to ignore the voices in my head. The need to kill was stronger, and I didn't know how much longer I could hold off to find the right guy. I needed someone with a muscular physique. The problem was the inn had been quiet the past few days. Weather was calling for snow, and I didn't want to take the chance of getting stuck behind the barn. My car wouldn't go down that path very well if Mother Nature decided to dump a good amount of snow.

I browsed the register, looking at the guests who had booked for the night. There were some couples, and one single man who had booked for two nights. Max Dubois. He could be the one. He had a late check-in tonight, which meant in all likelihood he wouldn't see the other guests. The cocktail hour would be done before he arrived. This could be a perfect situation…if only I knew what he looked like before he got here. The one thing that bothered me about these killings was that they were always sporadic instead of planned out.

I had made up a fresh batch of belladonna. I was itching to use it and finishing what I had started. Really two more men was all I needed. Maybe then I would be able to move away from this area. I had read in my father's journal that my parents had planned to move to a different state. My father had mentioned that there had been a detective sniffing around, but that was right before they had been killed in a boating accident. I didn't remember any detective coming to the house after the one day they showed up to inform my brother and me that our parents were dead.

The police must not have had any real leads as there was never anyone asking to search the property. Lucky for me apparently. From what I had read, my parents had killed at least twenty women. No wonder they wanted to move on. With kills that high, someone had to be doing some digging into all those missing people. They were smart though. I smiled at the thought of finally feeling connected to my parents, even if it was a twisted sort of connection.

The afternoon passed quickly with the checking in of all the guests, except Max. The cocktail hour went just as fast as the guests had a drink, but did not stick around to socialize, which was fine with me. The less people that knew when Max checked in, the better. I still wasn't sure if he was the one I was looking for, but I was hopeful. After Ramsay cleaned up from the cocktail hour, both he and Minnie decided to go to a movie. Relief flooded me at the thought of at least a couple of hours alone. Hopefully, the last guest would show up before they returned, and no one would be any wiser if he had actually checked in or not.

I did what little paperwork there was for the customers already checked in while I waited for my mystery single man to show up. Time passed slowly. It always did when I was anticipating a fresh kill. Hours came and went, with the guests returning and retiring to their rooms. Ramsay and Minnie got back from the movies and went to their rooms as well. I sat there at the registration desk, wondering what had happened to our last guest who had yet to show up. I allowed an hour to go by before I got up to lock the door. It was currently after ten o'clock and typically we only allowed people to check in until nine p.m.

I locked the door and straightened up the living room off the foyer, putting away magazines that some of the guests had been perusing during the cocktail hour. I switched off lights and stood in the dark at the front window overlooking the parking lot. There was no movement in the dark, no new cars arriving. I sighed and turned toward bed. Another wasted opportunity.

I was up with the sunrise and took my coffee out on the deck. It was a chilly morning, but bundled up in my heavy jacket with gloves on, the crisp air felt good. I didn't last very long out on the deck, but it was enough to jump start my day. With a second cup of coffee, I headed to the registration desk. Our missing guest had booked for two nights, so there was always the chance he would still show up today.

Most of the guests had either checked out completely, or had gone out to explore. I was finishing up some paperwork at the registration desk when the door opened. I glanced up and there he was. It had to be Max. And my, he definitely worked out. He would be the perfect specimen.

"I'm Max Dubois. I was supposed to get here yesterday, but I had a slight emergency come up."

"Welcome, Max. No worries. I was wondering if you would turn up, but at least you've gotten here now."

I updated his registration and handed the room key to Room 1. "I think this is the best room in the house." I smiled.

He nodded. "Great. I've got a couple of errands to run, and then I'll be back. Thanks so much."

"Don't forget about the cocktail hour tonight."

He nodded as he turned and walked back out the door. I frowned. Running errands? Does that mean he knows people here? How familiar is he to this area? This one could be a bit tricky, but I felt the pressure of finishing my plans and didn't feel like letting this one go. Time would just have to tell if I was taking a bigger risk than I thought.

I was sitting in the living room when Max returned. I was going through the books that had been on the bookshelves as I switched them out every few months just for a change of pace. Not that the guests usually read them, but I would read them if I had some quiet evenings, and I got bored with what was on the shelves now.

"Welcome back." I smiled warmly at him. He gave me a quick nod and headed to his room. I scowled. Not very friendly. It would be difficult to get a conversation going with him.

I finished reshelving the books and picked up the ones to return to the storage closet for future use. I had the itch to see blood run down spikes and wanted this evening to get here quickly. I sighed, thinking of the hours ahead of me, the need to make small talk with the guests, needing to slip Max some belladonna…yes, the night was going to drag by. Yet, a smile appeared as I anticipated the look in his eyes that moment he realized he couldn't move, and that he was in danger.

Danger. It was a strange word. How does one realize they are in danger, especially if people around them don't appear dangerous? I closed my eyes imagining the look in his eyes, the fear. The rest of the afternoon went quicker than I expected, and as Ramsay set up for the cocktail hour, I busied myself with minute details, staying in the kitchen as much as possible. I slipped my bottle of belladonna into my pocket. Hopefully there would be an opportunity to give Max my special ingredient in his drink.

Max appeared shortly after the rest of the guests. He mingled a bit, and then moved off to the side. He seemed content to be people-watching and keeping to himself. I made my way through the guests, talking with them about their day and what their plans were on check-out tomorrow. As I finished talking with everyone else, I made my way to Max.

"Enjoying yourself?"

He nodded. "I am considering…"

I glanced at him quizzically. "Considering?"

"I'm not a people person. I much prefer to be myself." He shrugged.

"I understand that. Sometimes after these cocktail hours, I just want to lock myself away. It can be exhausting always interacting with people." It was the most I had ever said to anyone about how much of an introvert I was. "What are your plans tomorrow? More sightseeing?"

"No. I'm headed home. I was here just on business really, but I got everything tended to this afternoon while I was out." It was a vague answer and for some reason it rubbed me the wrong way. People didn't tend to be so secretive when they were talking about vacations. But he had said business…which took me back down the path of wondering if he was familiar with this area and if someone would actually miss him when he didn't get back home.

He didn't contribute any further information and the silence was brutal. I moved away to talk with Ramsay as the guests were finishing up their drinks. Max continued to stand off to the side, and when one of the other guests went over to him, they talked in earnest. I was curious as to the conversation, but couldn't stare at him and even get closer without looking too obvious.

Finally, the cocktail hour seemed to be over and

most everyone had left. Max was standing at the bookshelves perusing the books.

"Anything in particular you like to read?" I asked.

He glanced over to me and shook his head. "Just looking them over."

"Well, they are there for the guests' use. Feel free to take one and read it, if you would like."

"I'm honestly just beat. Am thinking I'm going to crash early tonight and get an early start in the morning."

I nodded, puzzled by this man. I didn't want this one to get away, yet I could find no reason to offer him another drink, laced of course with my special ingredient. I proceeded to pick up dirty glasses and take them to the kitchen as Max continued to look through the bookshelves. When I came back in the living room, he had a book in his hand, reading the back cover.

"Found one that caught your interest?"

He smiled. "This was always one of my favorites. Basically, the one that got away and learning how to find the right one when there are plenty of fish in the sea."

I forced my face not to reveal my disgust. "Not sure I've read that one."

"It's pretty good." He shrugged before he put the book back on the shelf. "I'm going to head to my room, don't want to be in your way."

"You're not in my way. Feel free to stay and relax. I'm just picking up the last of the glasses. I'll be in and out, but enjoy the quiet without isolating your-self completely." I went back to the kitchen as quickly as I could. I hoped he stayed in the living room. I slid my hand in my pocket to make sure my bottle of my belladonna was still with me and headed back to the registration desk. Max was sitting on the couch reading the newspaper that had been on the coffee table. I didn't speak to him, but started printing bills that I would slip under the guests door before their check out.

Max approached the desk. "Would it be possible to get a glass of water?"

"Of course, let me get that for you." I rose and went to the kitchen, concealing my inner elation. This was going to work out perfectly. I grabbed one of the green-colored glasses from the cabinet. The light color to the liquid would not be seen through the colored glass. I filled it with water and added some drops of the belladonna to it.

I handed the glass to Max. "Anything else I can get you?"

"No, thank you. This is great. See you tomorrow." He moved toward his room, and I sat down at the desk.

The house settled, and before long, it was quiet. Minnie and Ramsay had both gone to bed. I sat at the desk, waiting for the right time to go to see Max. He was ready, I just knew it. I grabbed the special box with the beautiful fishhook in it and the key to Room 1. I unlocked the door and slowly opened it. The room was dark and I could make out the shape of Max's body in the bed. I walked quietly to the bed and looked down at him. The water was gone and he was sleeping. I gently ran my fingers over his bicep.

The power that came through even in slumber surprised me.

He opened his eyes and tried to speak. I put on the small light on the bedside table and watched him as he realized what was happening. "Don't panic." I smiled down to him. "I have a surprise for you." I withdrew the fishhook and pulled his mouth open. I pushed the barbed end through his cheek and smiled as the pain flashed through his eyes. I gave it a slight tug. "Always about the fish in the sea, isn't it?" I whispered.

His eyes searched mine, pleading with me. I knew he wanted to know why, but instead I just smiled at him. I had waited so long for this one. I leaned over him and kissed his forehead. "It was a pleasure to meet you, Max," I said as my left hand hit the button behind the headboard. His bed dropped to the side, and Max fell. I watched, fascinated as his body hit the spikes, blood immediately running down the spikes and onto the floor. He didn't move. He had hit the spikes perfectly, killing him instantly.

twenty-seven

Dawson picked up his phone and dialed Kathy's number. His favorite person at the State Police Headquarters. She had a flare for making life seem so easy. She was a voice he could talk to every day and still never have a complaint about her.

"Whatcha ya need, handsome?" Her chipper voice came across the line.

"I figured you had forgotten who I was at this point, it's been so long since we talked." Dawson responded.

"Never forget you. But it is a bit tedious only hearing from you when you need something."

Dawson smiled. "I know, Kath. I promise I will do better."

"But..."

Dawson chuckled. "You never fail to see right

through me. I have this lead, if you can all it that, that I need to be looking at some cold cases. Can you pull any unsolved murder or missing persons cases from this area… Maybe a 100-mile radius?"

"Of course. It's going to take me a little bit, but I'll get it to you as soon as possible."

"You are the best, Kathy. I owe you." Dawson ended the call.

What now? He was in a waiting pattern until Kathy found the files he needed. He pulled the stack of files in front of him closer. He would start with the few missing people files he had left.

Dawson's phone rang, and when he glanced at the caller ID, he saw Kathy's number. "I hope this means you found something."

"Do I ever let you down?" Kathy asked.

"Never."

Kathy chuckled on the other end of the line. "I think I have something for you, but they are odd cold cases. I'm emailing the files to you."

"Thanks. What do you consider odd?" Dawson asked.

"Every single one of the fifteen files I'm sending you are women who all disappeared after going out on the town for a girls' night in the same area. It looks like police had canvassed the bars in the area, but every single case went cold."

"I'll check them out. Anything that would indicate they're related to today's murders?" Dawson asked.

"Not that I could see, but that is why you get paid the big bucks." Kathy chuckled as she hung up the phone.

The cases that came through from Kathy were

enough to make Dawson cringe. Not only were there more than twenty of them, but they were all almost identical. All the girls missing were about the same body build, same color hair, and all had been last seen out with the girls, bar-hopping. Dawson didn't see how they could all be cold cases. All the same area. Was no one investigating at all?

He started scanning through files on the computer. It was going to be a long night. Each file had to be gone through meticulously. It was tedious and time consuming, but he made a list of all similarities, whether they were helpful or not. These files lacked detail. They were decades old and had been handwritten or typed old-schooled on a typewriter. They had later been uploaded to the computer when things went digital, but as far as the ease in going through the files, it was a nightmare.

All the cases seemed to follow the same pattern. The girls were out with a bunch of girlfriends, bar-hopping. The missing girl would leave because she wasn't feeling well and would take a cab home. That seemed to be the end of it until one of the girls tried to reach her a few days later, and then the missing person's report was filed.

All bars had been investigated. Bartenders or servers stated they remembered the group of girls, but not any of the individual ones. There had been only a handful of cab companies between all the areas, and none of them showed any pickups at a bar on any of the nights in question. Dawson started looking into who would have owned a yellow vehicle in the areas, but that produced very little.

By the time midnight rolled around, Dawson had a map on the table that had a mark for every spot a girl had gone missing. Drawing a circle around the area, he found the center to be in the town of Lyme. Lyme was pretty rural with lots of land. He needed a couple of hours of sleep before he headed that way.

Can you send me names and number of acres of people who live in Lyme? Anything over 5 acres. He sent Kathy a text, hoping that by the time he was ready to go in the morning that she would have the information he needed.

Dawson tossed and turned most of the night and by four a.m. he was wide awake, although feeling groggy as anything from lack of sleep. He took a lukewarm shower to try and wake up and was making coffee when his phone beeped.

Check your email. There isn't a lot, but it should give you enough to start with. I know you are up and probably have coffee in hand.

Dawson smiled. He swore Kathy never slept. He pulled his laptop to him at the kitchen table and opened his email. There were six listings of properties that were over five acres in Lyme. He printed off the listing information and glanced at his watch. It was now five-thirty a.m. By the time he got to Lyme, it wouldn't be an unreasonable hour to start talking to people.

He shot off a text to Ali: *Headed to Lyme re cold cases.*

Be careful. Love you. Ali was already up and working also. Dawson shook his head, neither of them slept much when dealing with a serial killer.

twenty-eight

Dawson had done some research, and after the talk with the past-life person, he was no closer to solving these cases than he had been before all this. He mentally rolled his eyes. This particular case was wearing him down. The chief kept insisting he should be working with the psychic. However, Dawson had avoided any contact with her as much as he could. His gut told him that she would just lead him away from where he needed to be searching, and he couldn't waste that kind of time.

The chief met Dawson at the door when he arrived that morning. "Dawson, just the man I've been waiting for."

Dawson smiled, but inwardly cringed. He knew where this was going, but there seemed no way out at the moment. "What do you need?"

The chief gestured toward his office. "Not what I need, but what *you* need."

"Excuse me." Dawson walked into the chief's office and stopped short. There was the psychic with a smug smile on her face. Dawson's irritation flared. He hated having to fight with a local department when they insisted on butting into his investigation.

"Detective Dawson, I fear you have been avoiding me." Cheryl's words were so laced with sweetness, Dawson wanted to bolt from the room.

"I haven't been avoiding you. I've been working on solving the recent murders. That doesn't leave a lot of time for idle chitchat." Dawson glanced at the chief. "I have a lot to do, and I really don't appreciate you trying to push your agenda on my case."

The chief looked at Dawson, his eyes veiled of any emotion. "Not pushing any agenda. You're obviously having trouble getting leads, and this is a good opportunity for a breakthrough, wouldn't you agree?"

"Actually, I disagree. This is a State Police matter, and I appreciate the use of your station for me to work out of, but I will not be bullied into using a *psychic* in this case when I feel it is irrelevant."

"You might as well sit down, Dawson. I spoke with your supervisor this morning and he gave me the go-ahead to arrange this meeting and to let you know that you need to be working closely with Ms. Porter."

"Well, although I appreciate the gesture," sarcasm dripped from Dawson's words, "I have an appointment, and this isn't a good time." Dawson turned toward the door to leave. He paused at the doorway and glanced back at the chief. "And don't worry about calling my boss, I'll be on the phone with him within seconds of leaving this office."

Dawson headed for the conference room, grabbed two files on the table and his laptop, and made a beeline for the door. He wasn't about to sit in this office and be manipulated by the local chief. Anger boiled within him, and he knew if he didn't get out of the building, it would explode onto someone unsuspecting.

He had no sooner left the station before he had his phone in his hand and dialing his boss's number.

"I know what you are going to say," Trent Samuels said before anything else.

"What are you doing? You know this is my case, and I don't like the locals butting in." Dawson's irritation made the words a bit harsher than he intended.

Trent chuckled. "Don't I know it. However, hear me out. We've used a couple of psychics in missing person cases, and they have helped. I know you're a skeptic about all this stuff, and I'm not saying you have to work with her—"

"Really?" Dawson broke in. "Because that wasn't the message that was given to me from supposedly you."

Trent sighed. "I know. I do think it's a good idea for you to at least talk with her in depth. You don't have to work with her every day, but at least have a conversation with her." Trent paused. "You need a break, Wes. I know this. After this case is solved, it might be important for you to take some time to yourself."

"Is that an order for me to take time off?"

"Of course not. Wes, I've known you a long time. You get immersed in your cases, which is a good thing, but it also takes a toll on you. I don't want you burning out because of these tough serial-killer cases. You're the best we have to work on them."

Dawson exhaled slowly, letting the irritation go. "Thank you. I appreciate you saying that. I will have one conversation with her, but I won't allow her to steer this case in a different direction. I have some leads I'm following up on, and they could be promising."

"You are in charge. You know my suggestion, but I also know that you trust your gut and it typically works for you. Go solve this mess, and we'll talk after. Let me know if you need anything from this department. Kathy is digging for more information for you, but if you need anything else, just call."

Dawson hung up the phone without another word. He should have known that Trent wouldn't be insisting he use the psychic, but for whatever reason, everyone seemed to think it was important for him to at least have a conversation with her. He scowled. One conversation…that was it.

Dawson had made it to his car while on the phone with his boss. He leaned against the car, thinking about Trent's *suggestion* of having one conversation with this psychic. He shook his head. He balked at the very thought of it, but also knew that Ali would be telling him to do this…that there would be no harm from it.

"Detective Dawson?"

He looked up and saw Cheryl walking toward him. He groaned silently. He should have gotten in his car and been out of there before she came out. "Yes?"

"I know you don't want to work with me. I get it. You're not a believer in how psychic ability can be useful, however, I do wish we could talk. I think you'll find it extremely useful, not just for the case, but for you in general."

"I appreciate that, but—"

"No buts." Cheryl smiled and handed him her business card. "Here's my cell phone. Think about it and call me. We can talk wherever you want. Chief Harris doesn't need to be involved."

"Wait a second." Dawson sighed. "Fine, I'll talk with you, but I'd like to do it somewhere else rather than here." He wrote the address of a coffee shop in Leighton on the back of her card and handed it back to her. "Say, three this afternoon?"

Cheryl glanced down at the address. "I'll be there."

twenty-nine

Dawson arrived at the coffee shop in Leighton. He had already asked Ali to join him, and once she heard that there was a psychic coming to talk to them, she readily agreed. He ordered two coffees and sat down to wait. He had no sooner sat down when Ali walked through the door. She had her hair in a ponytail, which always gave her a youthful look.

She slid into the chair next to him and picked up her coffee. "Thanks." It was just one word, but Dawson heard the appreciation in her voice.

"Long day?"

She nodded. "And it's not over yet."

"I didn't mean to take you away from it."

She reached for his hand. "Please. This is a welcome break. Besides, I'm intrigued with this psychic thing. I thought you were dead set against it."

He shrugged. "Even my own boss thinks at least one conversation should be had with her."

Dawson raised his hand and caught the attention of Cheryl as she came through the door. He stood as she walked over to the table. "Can I get you something?" he asked.

"No, thank you. I'm good." She pulled out a chair and sat.

Dawson sat back down. "This is our medical examiner, Ali Jenson."

"Cheryl Porter."

Dawson leaned back and waited. She had wanted this meeting, and he wasn't inclined to start the conversation.

Cheryl smiled. "I can tell you're a skeptic, but I hope that you'll find this information useful."

"Where did you get *this* information?" Dawson asked.

"I had a vision. The visions sometimes are shadows, not always clear, but other times they are *very* clear."

"And do your visions tell me who the next victim might be or even better, who the killer is?" Dawson tried to keep the snarkiness out of his voice.

Ali put her hand on his arm and squeezed. He knew this was her way of telling him to not bait the psychic.

Cheryl didn't even react—a sure sign that she was very used to people not believing in her abilities. "It's not that easy, detective. I have felt coldness when I had the visions, which would lead me to believe the bodies have been killed or stored in a cold environment, freezer, or something of the like."

Dawson nodded. "And the chief could have told you the ones we recently found were in a freezer."

Cheryl smiled. "Just to be clear, Chief Harris has not said a word to me about the details of the case."

"As well he shouldn't." Dawson frowned. "What did you mean when you said to look to the past?"

"There seems to be a connection to this case to something in the past. Again, I don't have any specifics, just a feeling of a connection." She raised her hand. "Before you start saying it's nothing and I can't help you, please hear me out."

Dawson nodded, and he could still feel Ali's hand on his arm. It was simply resting there, but it was enough pressure to make him aware of her support, and allowed him to relax. Whether he wanted to hear this or not, he knew Ali was fascinated.

"Something else has come to me that has nothing to do with this case." Cheryl watched Dawson carefully. "Are you estranged from a family member?"

Dawson narrowed his eyes. "Why?"

"I just have this feeling that there is someone you were close to, who you haven't been able to talk to, and you are looking for them."

Dawson felt Ali's eyes on him, and he turned toward her and met her gaze. He searched her eyes, looking for something that would either give him hope or let him know this woman was playing with him. Ali nodded at him, the encouragement he needed in her eyes.

"Yes." He faced Cheryl again. "I've been looking for my sister. Why are you, so called, *feeling* something about her?"

Cheryl leaned forward, intently eyeing Dawson. "She doesn't want to be found, detective."

"I figured that out since she has left me notes telling me to stop searching for her. This isn't exactly news to me." He scowled.

"She doesn't want to be found, but that doesn't mean she doesn't need you. She's going to need you shortly, whether you want to help her or not."

"What does that mean, whether I want to or not?" His agitation came through his words, and he clenched his fist. It caused his arm to tighten under Ali's hand, and she moved it to gasp onto his hand, once he loosened his fist to allow it. She knew the connection he needed right then. Only Ali understood the roller-coaster of emotions that ran through him when it came to Sara. She was the only one who gave him the chance to vent and rant about Sara, and also understood how deep his love ran for his sister.

"I don't have the details, but the feeling is that you won't be happy with her."

"Impossible." Dawson shook his head. "So, is there nothing else you can give me for the actual case you wanted to talk about? My sister is off limits."

"I have nothing definitive. Just that there is a connection to the past, and whether the past or the present, there is a great deal of land involved."

Dawson shook his head. "Well, okay then. I guess that's it."

Cheryl stood. "I know you don't think this was very helpful, but I hope as you contemplate it, it will trigger something that will be useful."

thirty

It was a warm day, unusually warm for February in Connecticut. I sat out on the deck, my hands wrapped around my mug of coffee. There had been no guests last night and there were no reservations for the next couple of days. Consequently, both Minnie and Ramsay had taken a few days off.

I was alone and enjoyed every second of it. I opened one of my father's journals that I had brought home from the barn. I loved reading his entries. The details were right down to the most miniscule points.

This one was a young one. She had been with her friends for a bachelorette party. This is the first time I have taken one that could be missed so soon. She had been so drunk that she didn't even understand what I had been saying to her. I even told her how much I wanted her to feel pain and she laughed. She won't be laughing shortly when I see how much pain she can take before she breaks down and screams for mercy.

There had been a gap of time between that entry and the next one, which was obvious just from what my father had talked about.

This one had a high pain tolerance. She didn't want to give me the pleasure of screaming in agony. But with the use of my favorite device, she screamed and screamed, begging me to stop. I couldn't help but laugh at her. The patheticness of thinking that I would just let her go home. Who thinks that way when shackled to a wall? She finally begged me to kill her and I was tired of listening to her whining so I gave her exactly what she wanted...a quick, bloody death.

I was jolted out of my reading by the bell ringing on the registration desk. I glanced at my watch. Time had passed by while I was reading, and I hadn't realized that it was now close to six p.m. I stood and made my way inside.

"May I help you?" I asked the young gentleman at the desk.

"Yes, sorry to bother you. Do you have any rooms available?" He looked around as he spoke.

"We do. Although some of our staff has the day off so there won't be a cocktail hour like there normally is." I set the journal down in the shelve below my desk.

"That's fine. I'm just looking for a place to stay for the night. I've got a long drive ahead of me tomorrow." He handed me his credit card. *Brett Jenkins.*

"Mr. Jenkins, glad we could accommodate you. You will be in Room 1, right here." I gestured to the door beyond the registration desk. "Is there anything else I can get you?" I looked him over as I handed back the credit card. The man was in great shape.

"Is there any way I can get some water? I'm just going to grab my bag from the car."

"Would you prefer something a bit stronger? A beer maybe?" I smiled at him.

"That would be perfect. I very much appreciate it."

I watched the man walk to the door. His legs were muscular and filled out his jeans perfectly. He would provide the final piece that I needed, then I could put all this behind me and start a new life.

I went to the kitchen while he was outside and prepared the beer for him. We were there alone tonight, just the two of us, and I tingled with the anticipation of my final piece.

I waited in the kitchen until I heard Brett come back inside and go to his room. I then went to his door and knocked. When he opened it, I held out the beer. "You're welcome to come out and talk. I'm just finishing up some paperwork."

He shook his head. "Thank you, but I've gone some things to do for work, and then I'm going to relax. Thanks for the beer."

I nodded as he shut the door. I moved to the registration desk and sat down. There could be a problem with this one. He obviously was working, so he probably had a computer and his car was there. Usually, I could dispose of the car and make it back to the inn before I was missed. With no one else there, that wouldn't be an issue. The issue was where do I leave *this* car? I had left some in the woods twenty miles or so away from the inn, but I couldn't really leave another one there. I needed it to be totally gone somewhere, and with the lakes still frozen, I couldn't just drive it into the water.

I sat back. I needed to find somewhere I could get the car to go over a cliff and into the ocean. That might work, but I would need to have his stuff in the car when it happened.

It was really a stroke of luck that I was there alone. No one would even know he had been there. I hadn't put his card in the system, but he didn't know that. There would be no trace of him ever being there.

I waited another hour before I picked up the box that contained a fishhook and headed to his room. I listened with my ear pressed against the door—no sound came from inside. I unlocked the door and quietly swung it open. He was lying on top of the bed, sleeping. The poor man. He must have been so tired that he couldn't even get undressed. His computer was lying next to him on the bed with some papers scattered on top of it.

I crept over and reached for the papers. They looked like some sort of legal documents. Was he a lawyer? Not that it mattered, but none of my other victims had really given me any clue as to what they did for a living. I was curious, but my blood rushed with the urgency of the kill. I progressed around the bed and lifted the beer bottle. It was empty. I gathered the papers and took his computer off the bed and placed everything on the table. When I went back beside him, I saw that his eyes were open. He had already realized he couldn't move. His eyes held no fear, just anger.

"You can't possibly be mad at me, Brett," I sweetly said. "You are the perfect ending to my masterpiece."

He tried to speak, and I smiled. "Don't try talking. It won't work, and you will just get angrier." I reached for the box and pulled out the hook. "I chose this one just for you. Technically, I don't have to give this one to you, but there's just been too many of you thinking there are more fish in the sea. Yes, yes, I know you didn't say that, but you just look the type." I showed him the hook with the bright green feather attached to it. He looked at the feather, and then to me—his eyes a flurry of questions. The emotion that poured through those eyes. I almost hated to do this to him. *Almost.* I ran a finger down his cheek. "Don't worry. It will all be over soon."

I gently cupped his chin and pulled down. I pushed the barb through his cheek and hooked him. I gave it a little tug for good measure, and his eyes again filled with anger. The pain was there, too. I could see it, as much as he tried to hide it. The man put up a good front. The others all had been so scared. I admired this one. He was strong, and that was something I had been looking for.

"I wish this could have been different," I whispered and pushed the button. The bed fell, and in an instant, Brett was hurling toward the spikes, waiting for him just below. Spikes pierced him with a dull thud as his body impaled itself. I repositioned the bed. I opened his laptop, but it was password protected. *That's okay.* It would end up in the ocean, somehow, with his car and all his belongings in it.

I made my way down the stairs to the room below. When I walked in, the blood was running like little rivers down the spikes and to the drain on the floor. The flowing red river mesmerized me. Strange how the headache never hit me with this one. I realized it as soon as I was down in the basement looking at the body.

His perfectly formed legs had been untouched by the spikes. I lowered the spikes and allowed his body to sit on the floor, then opened a tarp and rolled the body onto it. This had become routine, and I'd grown skilled at my technique. I wrapped him and placed him in the bag that was ready and waiting for him. It wasn't long before I had him out to his car. I returned to the house to collect his belongings and to lock up before taking him and his car to his final resting place.

I arrived in Lyme in record time. There had been no traffic, and I was able to drive out behind the barn with no problem. Once depositing his body in the freezer with my fifth victim, Max, I locked up the barn again and headed back to the inn. I would find a spot closer to the inn to have his car drive over the cliff to the ocean. It would be a while before they found it, at least until some warmer weather when boats were about, but by then, I would be long gone.

thirty-one

I pulled from the shopping bag the two large needles I had bought as well as the black nylon spool of thread. This would be just perfect. I lined them up on the bench next to the saw I had brought with me. After the cannery fire, I had decided to bring my lovely men here—the last three to finish my creation. My darlings: Kevin, Max, and Brett, would be the final pieces.

I switched on the radio as I started to prepare to get to work. Inside the freezer was an inverted table. I had locked it approximately half upright. There sat the new love of my life.

I used a skull that I had dug up on one of my many nightly adventures and molded clay around it to shape the face. With the skin of Darren's face, my man started to take shape. Charlie's bright-blue eyes stared back at me, and I smiled. In the back of the freezer were the bodies of Kevin, Max, and Brett. Kevin had already been harvested for his torso and ears, and I moved what was left of him aside. I pulled Max out to the workbench and laid him gently down on the tarp. I ran my hand lovingly up his arms. Those perfectly muscular arms.

I picked up the saw, started it, and listened to the hum for a few minutes. *Such a wonderful sound.* I closed my eyes and let the giddiness of anticipation roll over me. Slowly, I reopened them and knelt beside Max. I placed the saw at his right shoulder, and with a clean cut, I severed the arm from his body. I shaved down the body a bit so the skin would be hanging over the edge, allowing me to sew it on neatly. I repeated the same actions on the left arm. As I shut off the saw, I inhaled deeply. One more step closer to the end result.

I made two trips back to the freezer carrying an arm each time. The door had been left open to bring the temperature up a bit, not only to thaw the bodies for easier sewing, but also so my fingers wouldn't be frozen while wielding the needle. The excitement of *finally* getting my perfect man warmed me to the core.

I returned once more to the bench to thread my needle with the black nylon, and picking up the scissors and the spool of thread, I returned to the freezer. I hummed to myself as I aligned the right arm and started stitching the arm to Kevin's torso. It was time consuming sewing the body parts together, but time wasn't an issue for me. I had the day off, and I was determined to have this perfect specimen done before the end of the day.

I finished the arms and laid down the needle and thread. Just needed legs now. Was there anything he was missing? I ran my fingers over the body, starting at the scalp and working my way down, carefully looking at each body part I had so carefully chosen. *Almost there.*

I again dragged the body to the tarp from the freezer. Brett was my final piece. I pulled the remainder of his clothes off him from his lower body. All I needed was his legs for this.

And then I saw it. *Oh, my . . .*

He was so well endowed. "Brett, dear, would you like to donate another part of you for me?" I smiled as I ran my fingers over him. Yes, this would work out well.

I reached for the sharp knife on the bench and proceeded to remove the necessary parts. I applied saline to them and returned them to the freezer. This would be the last addition after the legs.

I returned to Brett's body and took up the saw again. The saw buzzed as I made the necessary cuts.

Dawson drove down the driveway of the Stillman's house. This house was frequently empty due to the owner being out of town most of the time. Dawson had learned that the parents had died in a boating accident, and the house had been left to their two children. The son was the one who traveled, and no one seemed to know what happened to the daughter. The property had been owned by the family for generations, and it was the most central part to where all the girls went missing. This had been the one property he hadn't gotten to the last time he was in Lyme.

As he exited the car, his eyes roamed over the yard. It had been neglected for years. Flower beds were overgrown with the flowers being choked out by the weeds. The house desperately needed paint. There were no cars in the driveway, but he ascended the stairs to the front door and knocked. He waited a couple of minutes before he knocked again.

As he had thought, there was no one home. He walked to the end of the front porch and took in the side of the house. A barn was just barely seen from his vantage point. He left the front porch to walk around the house. From the back of it, the mowed part of the lawn was probably a couple of acres before it continued into woods. The barn sat at the edge of the yard.

He walked across the lawn to examine the lock on the barn door. It looked brand new and certainly not the original lock. He wandered behind the barn and stopped short when he saw an SUV parked. It had been driven up from a small path. Dawson made a mental note of the plates before he headed back to his car to call for backup. He ran the plate and found it registered to a Patricia Styles.

Dawson had no sooner gotten the information back on the registration when another car drove in the yard. A young man exited the vehicle. He was impeccably dressed in a suit and tie. He walked over to Dawson.

"Something I can help you with?"

"Are you John Stillman?"

"Yes, sir."

"I'm Detective Wes Dawson. I'm following a lead about some missing person files. They brought me here. Do you know a Patricia Styles?"

"Yes, sir. She was my mother, Styles was her maiden name. Passed away a few years ago at the same time as my dad."

"And the car behind the barn that is registered to her? It's a new registration."

"I'm not aware of any car behind the barn. I'm typically traveling for business, and in fact, I've just arrived home from a two-month trip."

"Would you mind if I searched the barn? And maybe you can tell me when the new locks were put on?" Dawson gestured toward the barn, and they both started walking that way.

"There haven't been any locks put on the barn since my dad locked it up when we were kids. He used it as his workshop and didn't allow me or my sister out there. I honestly never went in after my parents died. Really didn't give it a thought. Honestly, I didn't deal with much of anything when they died. My sister, Olivia, did some of it, but I just continued with my own thing, traveling for work."

They reached the barn and Dawson gestured to the lock. "As I said, it's new."

John examined the front lock, looking very puzzled. "That's odd. I haven't been out here since the death of my parents. Who would have put a new lock on this?"

They walked around to the back door where they found a combination lock. This one looked as if it had been there for quite a while, but it was unlocked.

"This is open," John said. "I think this was the original lock my dad had." John turned toward the car. "I don't know who would have parked their car here, but like I said, I've been gone on business."

"Is it possible someone has been using the barn as a place to stay?"

"I suppose it's possible. I wouldn't know. I don't come out here." John shrugged.

"May I?" Dawson nodded toward the barn.

"Go ahead in," John said as he stepped back, and then followed Dawson into the barn.

Dawson opened the door and went inside the barn. There wasn't much out of the ordinary. It looked like it hadn't been used in years. He moved further in and started up the stairs to the hayloft. He reached the top step and stopped.

What the . . .?

Chains and shackles hung from the rafters, making the barn no longer *ordinary*. Dawson walked over and looked at them. Although rusty, they were heavy shackles that would have held the strongest of men in place. There were some hanging from the rafters, which he assumed would be for arms, and others nearer the floor attached to the wall for legs. He grabbed his phone and sent a quick text requesting a forensic team to come, punching in the address.

He turned and glanced around the loft. A cabinet in the corner had the door ajar. He walked over, opened it, and found an assortment of torturous devices from various time periods. He didn't recognize all of them, yet when he saw the pear of anguish from the medieval times, he knew that there was brutal sadism in the obvious crimes that had taken place here. There were other sharp instruments and gags that made Dawson sick to his stomach just by looking at them. He was never *amazed* by what he saw these days in any case. Some were more out there than others, but when dealing with killers, there was little that could faze him. However, thoughts of what likely had gone on here nearly sent him over the edge.

He made his way back to the main level of the barn and moved toward the tack room. The soft sounds of music filled the air as he moved into the room. He spotted an open trap door in the corner that allowed the music to penetrate the room. A hum of some sort drowned out the music. He moved closer to the trap door and peeked down. Light flooded the room, but he couldn't see anyone or anything, just a concrete floor. The hum stopped briefly before starting up again. It stopped once more and Dawson waited to see if it would resume. It didn't. Instead, he heard a voice talking, but the words were inaudible.

Dawson, gun held in front of him, crept softly and made his way down the steps. On the floor next to a worktable were two torsos. One had his arms cut off—the other, his legs and *manly* parts. Dawson shuddered. Both had the same puncture words on their bodies as well as a fishhook through their cheek. A saw lay on the table, still dripping blood.

Dawson descended farther down the stairs, moving without a sound. On the far side of the room, a door stood ajar. As he crept closer, the cold air grew stronger. This was obviously a refrigerator.

A female voice came from inside the refrigerator, talking softly, and Dawson couldn't make out the words. He heard someone coming down the stairs, and he glanced back. John Stillman stood at the bottom of the steps, looking around. His eyes widened, and he covered his mouth, stifling a gasp, when he saw the two corpses on the floor.

Dawson held a finger to his mouth to make sure he stayed quiet and gestured for him not to move. Dawson took a deep breath to calm his racing heart. He cleared his mind as the rush of blood was all he could hear for a second. Here he was, finally at the end of this case, or so he hoped.

Dawson eased toward the ajar door and pushed it fully open. With his gun held in front of him, he stepped into the doorway.

What the fuck!

A young woman was talking softly as she jerked a long, bloody needle through a man's leg, sewing it on to…onto *what*? Dawson shook his head when he saw the creation in front of him. It was the picture one got from reading *Frankenstein*, but the book couldn't have prepared him for this. The mismatch of body parts sewn together with black thread.

"Stand up with your hands in the air!" Dawson barked.

The woman looked over her shoulder. "What are you doing in here?" She turned back to her sewing, completely dismissing him.

"Stand up slowly," Dawson demanded.

The girl gradually laid down her needle and stood to face him.

"Olivia?" John said from behind him before Dawson could say another word.

"Hi, John. Didn't know you were home." She smiled at her brother.

"What are you doing?" He motioned to the creation behind her. His face was white, and his hand shook as he made the gesture.

"Oh, that's my perfect man. Isn't he great? I just need to finish with this last leg." She started to turn back around.

"Do *not* move," Dawson said and sternly waved a hand, telling John to step back. "Come this way out of the refrigerator."

Dawson heard shouts and nodded toward John to go get the backup that had arrived. Olivia stepped out of the refrigerator and looked at Dawson. "How did you find me?"

"Ironically, I wasn't looking for you, but was following up some cold cases that brought me here."

Olivia smiled. "Yes, my dad's work. No one had solved them all these years. Aren't you the clever one."

"Hands behind your head." Dawson moved in back of her as she placed her hands behind her head and handcuffed her. He was just finishing when two local officers came down the stairs. "Put her in the car for now and keep her brother out of the barn."

Dawson turned back to the refrigerator and walked inside. On the wall to his right was a diagram of a body with names written on different parts. Charlie was written for the eyes, Darren over the face, and so forth. They were all the names of the other victims they had found. On the arms was written Max, the legs were Brett, and the torso and ears were Kevin. The three corpses in the other room. At least they had first names. Once Ali ran DNA, hopefully they'd be able to easily identify the men and put even more missing persons cases to rest.

Dawson looked at the creation on the table in front of him. The arms were attached and only one of the legs. The perfect man she had said. This girl was a new kind of messed-up.

Dawson left the forensic team to do their thing as he started up the stairs and back outside. He saw Olivia sitting in the back of the police vehicle and her brother standing off to the side. He made his way over to talk to John.

"Did you know about this?"

"No, sir," John answered. "I've been out of town and really haven't talked to my sister much. I always text her when I'm going to be around to see if we can get together. She never even responds to me."

"She mentioned something about your father's killings and all the cold cases that I had been looking into were his. Do you know anything about that?"

John's face drained of all color. "*No. My father?* That can't be right."

"I'd like you to come to the station with me… Branford Station…to answer some questions," Dawson said.

"Of course, sir." John glanced at the police car and his sister. "Can I talk with her?"

"Maybe at the police station. Right now I need answers from her and you, separately."

John nodded and Dawson moved toward the car. Dawson gave instructions to transfer Olivia to the Branford Police car as he would be using their station for his interrogations. The locals seemed happy to release her over to him. However, not very happy when Dawson had them stay and secure the whole place. He would be returning to search the property for more victims from the father after he had had a chance to talk to Olivia.

thirty-two

Dawson went into the first room where John sat, waiting for him. He didn't say anything while he sat down and pulled some photographs from a folder. He spread them on the table. They were the pictures of Charlie Stone, Darren Weldon, and Thomas Levesque.

"Who are they?" John asked.

"These are the first victims of your sister. Notice the trophies she had taken." He pointed to each picture. "Eyes, scalp, and facial skin."

"Why are there hooks in two of them?" John asked

"I don't know the why. But I do see there is one that doesn't have a hook." Dawson sat back. "What can you tell me about your sister?"

John shook his head and sighed. "She always seemed a bit strange when she was little, but it was typical awkward stuff. I tried to keep in touch with her after our parents died, but like I told you earlier, she never responded to me. I tend to travel a lot with work and never really pushed it. Over the years, we've just drifted apart and really are more strangers now than anything."

"And what about your parents? Anything unusual about them that you remember?"

"Nothing," John said.

Dawson slid all the photos together and slipped them back into the folder. "Hang tight. I'm going to talk with your sister, and then you'll have a chance to speak with her."

Dawson moved on to the next room where Olivia was sitting, strangely looking very relaxed. Dawson squared his shoulders before he walked in.

"I was wondering when you were going to get around to come see me." Olivia smiled.

"This isn't a social call." Dawson drew out the photos and laid them out on the table. "Let's talk about these men."

Olivia scoffed. "Men…typical men that have no real appreciation for women."

"Meaning?"

"They all were so careless with their feelings and words regarding the opposite sex. They all had the attitude that women were disposable, and there were other fish in the sea."

"Is that why you used the fishhook in their cheeks?" Dawson asked.

"Clever, isn't it?" Olivia looked at the pictures. "All but this one. Poor Thomas, he hadn't really done anything wrong, except stating he knew Charlie had been there and that had been the last place Charlie had been before he disappeared. I couldn't let him leave after that."

"Where is this place that you couldn't let them leave? Where did you kill these men?" Dawson watched her for any emotion to come across her face. There was none.

"Oh, where I work. At the Lifeline Inn. I think you had been there one day and spoke to our chef, Ramsay."

"I don't recall talking to anyone named Ramsay."

"Oh, you wouldn't have known him as Ramsay. That was my pet name for him since he was a chef. His name is Jake."

Dawson nodded. He knew exactly the place. The owners were overseas and he had never gotten a hold of them.

"I don't know if you talked with Minnie that day…Zoey. She was the cleaning girl, but she kept to herself mostly."

"How did you kill these men? What are the puncture holes in their bodies?" Dawson asked.

Olivia sat back and smiled. "I killed them right there at the inn."

"How?"

"Let me tell you a little story, Detective. When I first got my job at the inn, I was doing a little exploring. The house was fairly normal. Nothing unusual until I went into Room 1. I was checking out the walk-in closet and tripped over a loose board. When I pried it open, there was a stairway down to the lower level, the cellar part of it. There's not a lot in the that level, but I was drawn to one particular area. I really can't give it justice by explaining it to you. You would have to see it."

"What was in that room?" Dawson ignored her coyness.

"A box that would bring spikes up out of the floor. There's a whole drainage system that I was able to watch the blood just disappear into. No one ever knew it was there."

Dawson watched her. "How did you get the bodies on the spikes?"

Olivia sat forward, leaning her elbows on the table. "I would love to show you." She winked at him.

Dawson shook his head. "What about your father? You mentioned something about his killings at the barn?"

"Done with mine so quickly?" Olivia shrugged. "I didn't know my father had been a killer until I found the barn and saw the shackles. Even then, it didn't really mean anything to me. But once I found his box of journals, the ones where he detailed everything he did to those women, and how my mother was involved…excellent reading. I finally felt like I belonged to the family I had always been a peripheral part of."

"And how does your brother fit into that?"

Olivia gave a small laugh. "He doesn't. Mr. Goody-Goody knew nothing about the kills. I haven't even really spoken to him in years. He always wants to meet, and I just blow him off. It's nice to know that he was always the outsider and not me."

Dawson stood and picked up the photos. He turned without saying a word to her and left the room. He looked back through a window and saw her laughing to herself. Dawson approached the chief who had been watching their conversation. "I want to take her to the inn so she can show me where these spikes are. There's more to it, and she's not giving up the information. She definitely wants the attention and feels the need to show us."

The chief nodded. "I'll send a couple of my officers with you to help."

Dawson nodded. "I'm going to let her brother speak with her for a brief moment before we go."

Dawson brought John to the room Olivia was in. He went inside the room with John, but stood at the door. No way would he leave the two of them alone together.

"Olivia, why?" John sat down at the table. He looked like he had aged ten years in the brief time between meeting Dawson at his house and being here at the station with his sister arrested.

"Why? John, he told me to."

John tilted his head. "Who told you what?"

"I don't know. The man...I could hear his voice. He was always telling me this is the one, do it. I had these flashes, and they would stop once I had killed."

"You sound like a psychopath." Disgust laced John's words.

"Really?" Olivia said. "You're part of this family, too. Don't you feel the need to kill just like Father and Mother did?"

"What are you talking about? They didn't kill anyone."

"Ask the nice detective to read Father's journals. They're quite graphic." Olivia leaned forward. "You might enjoy it."

Dawson stepped forward. "Enough." He held the door open as John stepped through without another word to his sister. A few minutes later, two local officers and Dawson were hustling Olivia out to the car to head toward the Lifeline Inn.

thirty-three

It was a silent ride to the inn—aside from the sound of Olivia humming to herself. Dawson kept glancing at her in the mirror. She was definitely an odd one.

They pulled into the parking lot. Once Dawson and the other officers got Olivia inside, the man, Jake, whom Dawson immediately recognized from their previous conversation, came out from the kitchen, along with a woman.

"What's going on?" Jake asked.

"Oh, nothing to worry about." Olivia spoke before Dawson had a chance.

"I'm sure you remember me, Jake," Dawson said. "I was here a little bit ago. Do you think you could get the owners on the phone, please?"

"I'll try. But they're about six hours ahead of us, so it will be pretty late over there."

"It's important," Dawson said and turned to Olivia. "Which room was it?"

Olivia smiled sweetly. "Room 1…always Room 1."

Dawson had all he could do not to swipe that grin off her face. Her attitude disgusted him. *I need a vacation* ran through his mind.

The two officers walked on each side of Olivia as she walked to Room 1. They got there just as Jake got through to the owners. "Sir, Mr. Connors is on the phone."

Dawson stopped Olivia and picked up the phone. "Mr. Connors, Detective Dawson here."

"Detective, what can I help you with? Did something happen at the inn?"

"Sir, I need to inform you that your inn has been the place where multiple murders have taken place. We'll need to close you down for at least a few days while we get a forensic team in here."

There was silence for a moment. "My wife and I will be on a plane tomorrow to be there. Is our staff all right?"

"I'm afraid we have taken Olivia Stillman into custody. Let's talk when you get back in the states. I'll leave my card with Jake here for you."

They disconnected and Dawson looked up to see Olivia glaring at him. "You better not have gotten me fired, Detective."

Dawson raised an eyebrow. "I'm pretty sure you have gotten yourself fired. Let's see this room."

Olivia led them into Room 1. The officers stood

next to her by the window as Dawson moved into the room. It was not a large room and held a bed with a night table next to it. A small chair was also on one wall. Dawson walked over to the closet and opened the door. He stepped inside, sliding his foot along the floor to see if he could find a raised area.

"I put that runner over it so no one would trip on it and be able to open it," Olivia said.

Dawson flung back the runner and found the trap door. He lifted the door and pulled out his flashlight to shine down the stairs. He stood and walked out into the room again. "How did you get the men down the stairs?"

"Oh, I didn't. It was much easier to have them on the bed."

Dawson looked at the bed, and then back to her. "What are you talking about? Walk me through how you would kill these men."

Olivia sighed. "It's really not rocket science, Detective. I would make sure the men had a special ingredient in a drink when they went to bed."

"What ingredient?"

"Belladonna. I would boil it down to a liquid, and then put some in their drink. They would drink it, and then go to bed. It usually took thirty to forty-five minutes, and then they would become paralyzed." Olivia walked to the side of the bed next to the table. "I would make sure when I came in to look at their glass or bottle, depending on what they had, to make certain they had drunk it all. Then I would wake them and enjoy how the fear filled their eyes when they realized they couldn't move."

Dawson stood next to her. He studied her and noticed the transformation in her face. Her eyes changed in color and brightness. It was like he was seeing a different person. "And then what?"

Olivia stepped back and moved to his other side. "Just run your hand behind the headboard there and you'll find a button. Once you push it, you'll see how the men died." She moved to the foot of the bed. Her face had a strange look to it, almost like she was excited, but at the same time almost trance-like.

Dawson carefully did as she said, and his hand found the button she mentioned. He pushed it. With a swoosh, the bed dropped to the side. Dawson shone his light down and it illuminated a cement floor with grooves in it. "And they just landed on the floor? That doesn't explain the puncture marks."

"Oh, dear. I must have forgotten to reset the spikes. You'll need to go down to that room. There's a box with a button on it that will raise and lower the spikes." She smiled at him as if they were just in a normal, everyday conversation.

Dawson's stomach clenched. He turned and pointed to the female officer. "Stay here with her." And to the other, "you come with me."

They ventured down the stairs, Dawson leading the way. When they got to the room, the lights came on automatically, and Dawson shut off his flashlight. He saw the box Olivia had mentioned on the bench and went over to push the button. The spikes rose from the tracks in the floor and stopped when they were at full position. Dawson walked over and looked up. Olivia was looking down at him, still smiling.

Spikes

"So they would be on the bed," he said to her, "and when you released the bed, they would fall onto the spikes?"

"Yes. Isn't it glorious? Sometimes they would die instantly and others did not. Those were the fun ones. They couldn't release themselves and the pain they felt." She closed her eyes, and her smile broadened as if she relished the memory.

"And then what?" Dawson asked.

"Well then, I would retract the spikes and take whatever body part I needed. I would then wrap them in the tarp and put them in a bag. The first one I put in an old well here on the property where I was going to burn them, but that was the first one you found. Apparently, the ground eroded, and the body ended up in the sea. I had to get a bit more clever after that. I found the warehouse that was empty, and until that car accident, you never would have found them."

Dawson watched her. She stood above him at the foot of the bed like a victor claiming her prize. It didn't matter that her hands were cuffed behind her back, she held herself like she was the champion. He couldn't put his finger on it, but as before, there was a change in the color of her eyes. As Dawson looked at her, he could swear it was like seeing two different people.

She smiled down at him again. "Do you have a message for the devil as I will be seeing him soon?"

Dawson frowned, processing her words. "*What?*"

Olivia threw herself over the end of the bedframe and flew through the opening. Her smile got bigger and her eyes closed just as she landed on the spikes. He looked away at the thud of her hitting the spikes and them piercing her body. She had landed almost perfectly on them. One of the spikes went through her throat, killing her instantly.

"Put them down." Dawson pointed at the mechanical box where the officer pushed in. It was excruciatingly slow as the spikes lowered and tore back through her body as they entered the floor. Dawson swallowed the bile that rose in his throat. He thought he had seen everything, but this was a first for him.

The officer above was watching down through the open floor. Her body trembled and she held her hand over her mouth. "Sir, I couldn't stop her. I didn't anticipate her jumping."

"It's okay. None of us expected it. Call Jenson at the medical examiner's office and get them over here." Dawson squatted down next to Olivia. Even in death, she had a grin on her face.

In the recesses of his mind, he remembered Ali telling him how Lavinia Fisher had jumped off the gallows to hang herself before it was time, and she had said similar words. He closed his eyes. Lizzie, Lavinia…were these ghosts really coming through these young women and making them do the killing? He couldn't believe it, and yet there was something that just rang true.

Ali arrived at the Lifeline Inn and made her way down the stairs to where she found Dawson squatting near the woman's body. Dawson seemed completely transfixed on the rivers of blood that flowed from the woman and into the drainage lines. Ali noticed the tracks where the spikes would raise and lower, and she shuddered. He glanced up when she put a hand on his shoulder.

"Hey." He stood up.

"You okay? I was filled in on what happened." Ali searched his face to judge his reaction.

"I don't know what happened. It was so fast." Dawson ran a hand across his face like he was trying to wipe away the cobwebs from his mind. "It was like...it wasn't her."

Ali frowned. "What do you mean?"

"I don't know how to explain it. Maybe there is something to these ghosts that we seem to be chasing from the past. Was Lavinia really here, or Lizzie with Beth?"

Ali put her hand on his arm. "Don't overthink it. All we can do is mark these murders as solved, and deal with her death. Why she chose to kill herself we will never know. But you'll need to notify her brother."

Dawson nodded. "I want to check her room here, too. She mentioned journals that her father had of all the killings he had done. I may be able to close some of those cold cases also if his journals give enough information."

"Dawson, you solved it." Ali smiled at him. "It's over."

"Why do I feel like it's just beginning then? There's something unnatural about this case, and maybe there was on the other one, but this one goes beyond the capability of understanding."

epilogue

Sara turned the volume up on the TV. A *picture of Wes was being shown. An amazing job from our own State Detective Wesley Dawson. Not only did he solve the recent serial killer murders, but he also solved more than twenty cold cases that with an ironic twist of fate brought him to the killer he was really after. Detective Dawson is a one-of-a kind specialist when it comes to stopping those killers. We can all rest easier knowing Detective Dawson gets the man, or woman as the case may be, that he is after.*

Sara stood in front of the TV, her eyes on Dawson's picture. Her heart swelled with the pride she felt for him, yet she dreaded coming face to face with this man that she no longer knew. He had been young when she left, and she had been avoiding him all these years. The last time she had seen him, he had been begging her not to leave him behind. She had been young and foolish, but had gone on to do good things, regardless of the road she took to get there.

She knew he was looking for her, but she couldn't risk everything by being in touch with him. He could destroy all that she had built up.

The vision faded as abruptly as it had started. Cheryl Porter sat back in her seat. This was the estranged family member that Dawson had told her was off the table. This girl, his sister, loved him deeply. Cheryl could feel the pride and the pain that overtook her body as she watched the news account. A reconciliation was coming. Cheryl could feel it, and an icy chill overtook her as she realized this would not be a welcome reconciliation, but one of necessity and insinuations.

about the author

E.L. REED moved to Tennessee after living in New Hampshire all her life. She has fond memories of the Maine coastline and incorporates the ocean into all her books. She has three grown children and is enjoying her empty nest. Her life has been touched and changed by her son's autism - she views life through a very different lens than before he was born. Growing up as an avid read- er, it was only natural for Emma Leigh to turn to creating the stories for others to enjoy. Emma Leigh continues to learn through her children's strength and abilities that pushes her to go outside her comfort zone on a regular basis. She has also authored romantic suspense, women's fiction and co-authored children's books. She shares her love for writing as an English Professor at a local community college.

For more information, please visit elreedauthor.com

ALSO AVAILABLE IN THE
MEMORIES OF MURDER
NOVEL SERIES

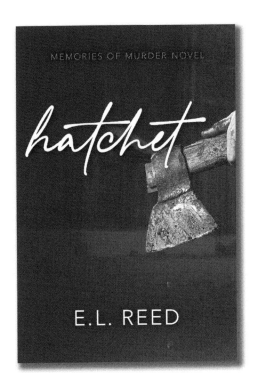

ALSO AVAILABLE AS AN AUDIOBOOK

ALSO AVAILABLE FROM
EMMA LEIGH REED

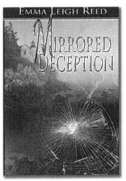

AVAILABLE WHEREVER
YOU BUY BOOKS

Made in the USA
Columbia, SC
16 July 2023

20092093R00130